The Duke's Scandal

A Regency Romance

Bluestocking Book Club
Book 5

Rose Pearson

The Duke's Scandal

Prologue

Isobella blinked back hot tears. "What do you mean by this?"

"It is what I have said." Lord Hogarth shrugged his shoulders. "I do not care for you any longer."

"But how can that be?" Isobella cried, her mother's hand settling on hers, though she quickly cast it aside and rose to her feet. "You and I are engaged! The banns have already been called!"

Lord Hogarth sniffed. "They have only been called twice. There is no need for them to be called a third time, not now that the engagement has come to an end."

Come to an end?

Isobella tried to breathe steadily, her chest furiously tight. How could this be? Their engagement had not been all that recent, but the courtship had been long enough – nearly three months. How could he not be certain? He had told her so many things, had promised her his heart, and yet now, here he was, telling her that it was at an end. And for what cause?

"Why would you end this engagement, Hogarth?" she

said, her voice hoarse. "If you have any care or consideration for me at all, then – "

"That is the concern," he interrupted. "I do not think I care for you any longer, as I have just said."

"But –but how can your heart change so quickly?" she exclaimed, "especially after you have shared so many things with me? You have told me how much I have come to mean to you, how glad you are that we met!"

Lord Hogarth looked away, a touch of pink in his cheeks. "I may have said all of those things at one time, but I confess that I did not truly mean them. My heart is not as I believed it to be."

Isobella, who had been standing tall to face Lord Hogarth, slowly sank back down into her chair, her mother still sitting there silently.

"I am sorry that I have caused you pain," he continued, speaking without any intonation whatsoever. "I shall take my leave of you now."

"She will be shamed!" Finally, Isobella's mother, the Countess of Granville, spoke. "The *ton* will speak of you both, but Isobella will garner just as much reproach as you! You may well tell them all that *you* are the one responsible for the ending of the engagement, but *they* will think poorly of her for it all the same! They will say that you were bored with her, that she was not interesting enough. Can you not see that?"

This did nothing to move Lord Hogarth. He stood precisely where he was, his hands clasped behind his back, his shoulders lifted, and his head held high as if, somehow, he was not in the least bit responsible for any of this. He said nothing whatsoever, did not even think to apologize, leaving Isobella to stare up at him, wondering if she had ever known him at all.

"How can you be so callous?" Lady Granville exclaimed, her voice echoing around the room now. "You have promised my daughter so much, and now you will not only take it all away but you will also damage her reputation with it!"

The tears that Isobella had held back for so long began to break through, dampening her lashes and beginning to fall to her cheeks. Her mother was right. She would not only have the loss of her engagement and her future, but she would also have her reputation damaged dreadfully. What would she do then?

"I am afraid there is nothing else for it but this," Lord Hogarth said, brusquely. "I must take my leave of you now. Good afternoon."

Isobella wanted to cry out, wanted to reach for him, to bring him back to her, but her body was too heavy, too weighted with grief. She closed her eyes and began to sob, her mother's comforting hand on her back.

The door slammed open.

"How dare you?"

With astonishment, Isobella lifted her head, seeing her brother storming into the room, his eyes wide with fury. Lord Hogarth began to back away, stammering furiously as Isobella clutched at her mother's hand.

"How *dare* you?" With fury burning in his eyes, Isobella's brother shoved Lord Hogarth back, preventing him from leaving the room. "How could you do such a thing?"

Isobella found herself on her feet. "What are you talking about, Granville?" Her brother had taken on the title some four years ago when their father had died unexpectedly, but since then, had been the most excellent brother. If he was behaving so towards Lord Hogarth, then Isobella knew it was for good reason.

"I have just heard what you have done to my sister!" Lord Granville exclaimed, gesticulating furiously as the Countess too rose to her feet. "The disgrace you have heaped upon yourself! The *shame* you have brought upon you both! The *ton* will say that my sister was not enough for you, that she did not hold your interest, and now – "

"Lord Hogarth was just about to take his leave, brother," Isabella said, softly, the heaviness in her body returning. "He has already informed me that he is ending the engagement because he no longer cares for me." She managed to keep her tears back with an effort. "He was just departing from this house, which I think might be beneficial for us all."

Her brother slid her a glance, but then looked back to Lord Hogarth. "Ah, but you did not tell my sister the truth about why you have chosen to end this engagement, I am sure. You have merely told her that your engagement is at an end because you do not feel the same way about her any longer... but that is not the real reason, is it? Now that I know the truth about you, however, I do not think that you have ever truly cared for my sister, have you? You have pretended, you have lied, you have feigned your interest, have you not? None of what you have told my sister, told my family, has been true, has it?"

"What do you mean?" Isabella blinked rapidly, seeing Lord Hogarth begin to back away from her brother, his hands held up defensively. "What is this about, Granville?"

Her brother's jaw tightened. "This is about Lord Hogarth pretending to be a gentleman when he is not. I am sorry for the pain you will and shall endure because of him, Isabella, but trust me, it is good that you will not marry him."

The tears in her eyes had faded away, her heart beating

furiously as she fought to understand all that was being said – and revealed – to her. One moment, she was filled with pain over Lord Hogarth's decision, and the next, confused by her brother's promise that it was a good thing for this all to end.

"I am afraid I have no desire to speak on this matter." Lord Hogarth drew himself up, but Isobella caught a slight tremble in his frame, as well as the way his eyes flicked towards her brother and back again. "The engagement is ended. That is all that matters."

Seeing her brother's eyes flare, Isobella held up one hand towards him, trying to get Granville to calm himself. "I do not think detaining Lord Hogarth any longer will do anything good," she said, her voice quavering. "We can speak once he has departed, can we not?"

Lord Granville glared at Lord Hogarth, refusing to move out of his way. For a long moment, both gentlemen stood facing each other, neither of them saying anything more. Isobella held her breath, her fingers twisting together as her mother stood beside her.

"Very well." His lip curling, Lord Granville stepped to one side. "And do not *ever* come near to my sister or think to set foot in this house again."

Watching him walk away, Isobella felt as if she were crumpling inwardly. This was the end of everything she had put her hope in for the last few months, the shattering of the dream she had built for so long.

"I do not understand," their mother said, sitting back down heavily. "This is the third gentleman who has disappointed you, Isobella. Your first Season, there was Lord Brookmire, who courted you but then stepped away, followed by Lord Pollock, who made so many promises as he begged to court you, only for him to elope to Scotland with another lady entirely!"

"And now this Season, I have found my engagement ended," Isobella murmured, rubbing one hand over her eyes before going to sit down again. "If I thought that last Season was disappointing, then this Season has proven to be even worse."

"It is worse than you know." Stalking across the room, Granville poured himself a small glass of brandy and, much to Isobella's surprise, poured another glass which he then handed to her. "I am overwhelmed with anger, I must admit. The moment I found out what he had done, my fury burned."

"Where did you hear it?" his mother asked, as Granville began to pace up and down the room. "It is only the morning and – "

"I was in Whites last evening," Granville interrupted, though not ungently. "There were some gentlemen gathered around the betting book. Naturally, I was interested."

Isobella shuddered, then lifted the brandy to her lips, taking a small sip of water. "I presume my betrothed's name was in the betting book?"

"He was." With another swig of brandy, Granville shook his head, looking away from her. "I spent the rest of the night – or the morning – looking for him. You can imagine my surprise upon returning home to be informed that he had come to speak with you, Isobella."

"Might you tell us what it is that you discovered?" With a sadness penetrating her voice, the Countess looked up at her son. "What did Lord Hogarth do?"

Granville scowled. "There was a bet in the betting book that said he would be able to... " His eyes slanted towards

Isobella and then back to their mother. "To *woo* the widower, Lady Cowden."

A weight dropped into Isobella's stomach. She did not need her brother to explain himself to know that this *wooing* would certainly have been more than that.

"The bet had been fulfilled last night," her brother finished, heavily. "You can imagine my feelings at that moment, I am sure."

Closing her eyes, Isobella cradled the glass of brandy in her hands before bringing it to her lips for another sip. This, then, had been the ultimate betrayal, and she had known nothing about it!

"I thought that he cared for me," she said, tears beginning to fall again. "He told me so. He said my heart was a precious gift, something that he would always value and cherish."

"He lied." The short, sharp truth from her brother made Isobella shudder violently, tears beginning to burn in her eyes again. "I am sorry to say it, Isobella, but nothing he said was true. He did not care for you as he promised, for he would not have behaved that way had he truly done so. I love my wife desperately, and there is nothing I would do to harm her. I felt that way when we were courting, and that feeling has only increased within my heart in the two years we have been wed."

Isobella swallowed hard. "That is what I had hoped to find for myself." She had seen the love shared between her brother and his wife, Louisa. Louisa had become more like an older sister to her, and Isobella had always been grateful for her friendship and her advice. "It seems I am never to find it."

"There is always next Season," her mother said, but Isobella did not let that fill her with any sort of hope. This was now the third gentleman who had failed to prove himself, the third and the most severe, given that they had been engaged.

"No, I think not," she whispered, unable to speak with any sort of strength now. "Mother, I think that there can be no hope for me now. The *ton* will speak of this for some time and I will be whispered about also."

Her brother closed his eyes, letting out a low mutter of frustration.

"It should not be that way," the Countess said, with tears in her eyes. "You have done nothing wrong, and yet, society will still whisper about you. Mayhap... mayhap we should return home and come back next Season."

Isobella threw back the rest of the brandy in what would be considered a most unladylike fashion, letting the heat of it push through her otherwise cold frame. Her mother was determined to come back next Season with her, to encourage her with such a promise, but Isobella knew her heart had shattered into pieces, pieces beyond repair. Her hope for a happy future with a gentleman who cared for her was quite gone, ruined now by Lord Hogarth and the other two gentlemen before him. It was never to be for her, it seemed. Fate was determined to cast her aside, to leave her alone and without a love and comfort of her own.

And all she could do was accept it.

Chapter One

Two years later

"I am delighted for you!" Isobella beamed with happiness and then hugged her friend tightly. "How truly wonderful for you both!"

Miss Sherwood smiled back at her. "I thank you," she replied. "Lord Suffolk has acted rather quickly, I must say, for we have not been officially courting for a very long time, as you well know!"

Isobella chuckled as the other ladies from the blue-stocking book club all came to congratulate Miss Sherwood. "That is true enough, but when you are as in love with one another as you both seem to be, I do not think that a particularly long courtship is required!"

"Indeed not, though the *ton* might wonder at it a little," Miss Trentworth grinned, a twinkle in her eye. "But you have nothing to prove to them, so why does it matter what society thinks!"

Lady Rosalyn smiled broadly. "Given that we are blue-stockings, we are all well used to ignoring society's expectations, are we not? So I am sure you can do the very same in this circumstance also, Eugenia."

Miss Sherwood tossed her head. "Yes, you are quite correct. I care nothing for what the *ton* thinks of our hasty engagement. Though I shall be sorry to leave London, for the banns are to be called very soon." She looked around the room. "There are to be so many weddings, are there not?" A sadness swept over them all, Isobella included. "We shall not be together again for some time."

"Unless," Lady Rosalyn said, quickly, "we all agree that we shall return to London every year, at this very time. We shall spend at least a month together – six weeks, mayhap? – and in that time, talk about whatever we wish, read whatever we wish – "

"And continue with our endeavors to solve whatever mysteries might be presented to us," Isobella interrupted, as her friends all smiled back at her. "I think that an excellent notion!"

Her friends all agreed at once, the atmosphere in the room light once again.

"Our husbands – or soon to be husbands – will enjoy having time together also, I am sure," Lady Amelia beamed, as a twinge of embarrassment began to overtake Isobella. "I think it is a wonderful idea, for I shall miss you all *very* much... even if we are all to be happily married!"

The moment she said this, Isobella's face flushed hot and her heart quickened. Lady Amelia's smile grew fixed, and she began to stammer, but Isobella smiled as quickly as she could, putting out one hand to her friend.

"Please, do not concern yourself," she said, warmly. "It was a mere mistake, that is all. You are not to be upset by this, Amelia. You know very well that I have no interest in matrimony but I shall be *very* glad to see you all married." This was said with as much conviction as she could put into her voice, hoping that they all believed her. Ever since Lord Hogarth had broken her heart, Isobella had silently determined not to let herself feel anything for a gentleman again. That meant she was not to think about matrimony, about love, or companionship. She was settled upon being a spinster – a bluestocking spinster, at that – which meant she had no upset at her own situation at present.

"I do apologize, Isobella." Lady Amelia came towards her as the other bluestockings fell into conversation again, blotting out the awkwardness that had followed Lady Amelia's remark. "I hope I did not hurt you."

"You did not, I assure you." Isobella smiled and pressed Lady Amelia's hand. "Please, do not worry. You are quite right, everyone else here *is* to wed... or shall announce their engagement very shortly!" As yet, not all of the bluestockings were engaged, but Isobella expected it very soon. Each one spoke of love and affection, of devotion and promise, and that, Isobella was sure, would lead them to happiness. "I do not mind being the only one unwed. I have already determined that I would not marry, so please, do not think poorly of yourself for speaking as you did."

This made Lady Amelia's eyes dim rather than look back at Isobella with any sort of relief. After another moment, she frowned, tilting her head one way and then the other, studying Isobella as if there was something in her expression that she could not make out. Isobella frowned, looking back at her friend and waiting for her to speak.

After some minutes, she did.

"I recall you telling me that I should pursue the chance of love between myself and Lord Broughton," she said, speaking in a low voice so that the other ladies would not overhear them. "You told me that even if there was not to be such a thing in the end, I would still be glad, one day, that I felt such an affection."

Isobella swallowed hard. "Yes," she admitted, quietly. "I did."

"And you spoke of a love you had once experienced," Lady Amelia continued, pushing Isobella gently with her unspoken questions. "The others do not know of this, I think."

Isobella let out a small sigh, her thoughts returning to Lord Hogarth. "No, the other bluestockings do not know. But yes, at one point, I felt such a deep affection, I believed that it was love. It was only the very beginnings of it, I think, but it still had a profound effect upon me. When it was taken away, when my heart was deliberately and painfully broken, there was nothing left within me but shadows and ashes. That is all that remains there now, I think." Her smile was sad, her heart beginning to ache. "I am glad for you all, however. I should not like you to think that I feel any sort of upset, jealousy, or even anger at your happiness."

Lady Amelia nodded slowly but still held Isobella's gaze. "I will repeat what I told you then, Isobella. If you ever wish to unburden yourself, then I should be glad to hear whatever you have to say."

With a small smile, Isobella embraced her friend, aware of the tears that began to burn behind her eyes, though she pushed them away quickly enough. "Thank you, Amelia. I have not spoken of it to anyone, not for over a year now." Stepping back, she lifted her shoulders and then let them fall. "I do not know if I need to do so, truth be told. My heart has settled, and I do not feel any further sadness."

Lady Amelia's eyebrows lifted. "Never?"

"No," Isobella stated, aware that she was lying not only to herself but also to her friend. "As I have said, I am more than happy for you all, but I do not need to search for such a thing for myself."

This made her friend's eyebrows draw low, but Isobella only smiled, hoping that Lady Amelia would not be able to see the truth in her eyes. There was still a lingering sorrow in her heart, a pain that did not ever seem to resolve. It stayed there, pushing deeply into the very core of who she was, reminding her, every time she saw happiness between a gentleman and a lady, that her own heart had been so utterly broken. The only reason she had returned to London was at the behest of her mother and the convincing of her brother, though she had made them both promise that she would be able to do as little or as much as she pleased when it came to society. That promise had been given, and thus, Isobella had pushed herself into the little group of bluestockings and had fully intended to stay there for the entirety of the Season. She had never once expected to find all of her friends now so happily engaged while she drifted on in solitude.

"You know that I am here to listen to you, to weep with you, to smile with you, or to simply sit with you, whenever you might wish it." Lady Amelia put out her hand and took Isobella's, squeezing it lightly as Isobella fought unexpected tears. "Do not hide your heart from us, Isobella. We are your friends, are we not?"

"You are," Isobella confirmed, hearing the hoarseness of her voice from the plethora of emotions that suddenly swamped her. "I am glad for that, truly."

Lady Amelia smiled, nodded, and then turned to ring the bell, ordering another tray of tea and cakes to be sent up. Isobella, on the other hand, retreated quickly, making her way from the others and going to one of the bookshelves near her, pretending to look through the books present. The library in Lady Amelia's townhouse was extensive indeed, but it was not the books that drew Isobella near. Instead, it gave her a place to hide herself, to regain her composure as the other bluestockings chatted and laughed together. None would think it strange that she had gone in search of a book, though soon they would all sit together again to drink tea and talk about matters of all kinds.

Isobella settled one hand against her stomach, trying to breathe more steadily. Her heart was still beating a little more quickly than before, her mind pulling up images of Lord Hogarth in front of her eyes. She could still remember the shock that had crashed over her when he had told her that their engagement was now broken, the pain that had sliced through her when he had confessed he did not care for her any longer. What had been worse, she considered, was the realization that she had begun to fall in love with a gentleman who had never truly cared for her, who had lied until she had let herself believe him. The trust she had placed in both him *and* his words had been shattered; her own willingness and desire to fall in love and to make her future joyous so great, it had dimmed any hint of doubt.

How much of a fool she had been!

They do not need to know of my shame, she told herself, recalling the words she had said to Lady Amelia some time ago. *I told Lady Amelia to pursue any chance of love and she did, and I am glad for her. I am only sorry that my own future did not permit me to have such joy.*

"We have to sit and discuss what we are going to do now that we have no mysteries left to solve!" she heard Miss Trentworth exclaim. "With everything just as it should be, does it mean that all we are left now to discuss is trousseaus and the like?"

The other bluestockings laughed, but Isobella's heart twisted painfully. She closed her eyes and drew in long breaths in an attempt to keep her composure. This was most unexpected, for she had never once imagined her heart responding in such a way! She ought to be quite contented at her friend's happiness, just as she had told Lady Amelia! So why now was she feeling such agony?

"Here is the tea tray," she heard Lady Amelia say, opening her eyes and forcing herself to smile as she turned around. "Come now, let us all enjoy some tea, shall we?"

Isobella went with the others to sit down, taking a cup of tea from Lady Amelia and smiling along with all that was said and shared between them. Trying to push away the lingering stabs of pain, she forced herself to listen to the conversation, to hear what was being said without responding to any of it. And yet, no matter how hard she tried, her heart cried out with all that she had endured already... and for all the loneliness that was surely still to come.

Chapter Two

"I have decided to go to London."

This proclamation made, Amos grinned at his mother as she gaped at him, fully aware that this was something she had been hoping to hear him say for some years now. He had taken on the mantle of Dukedom four years ago, and almost the very day his father had passed away, his mother had spoken about his need for a wife.

"You will, no doubt, try to keep me from stepping into the midst of society, but I must tell you, Mother, that I am quite determined!" Chuckling to himself at the scowl that drew into his mother's face at this remark, Amos could not help but continue his teasing. "I am certain you will warn me about all the dangers that lie there, about the many young lady that will try to drag my attentions towards them, about the gentlemen who will seek to befriend me solely because of my wealth and standing but, alas, I fear there is no other way for me to find myself a suitable bride unless I make my way there."

"Oh, Amos, do be quiet."

Amos turned, seeing his sister standing by the door of

the drawing room. He had not heard her come in. "Good afternoon, Flora." He tipped his head. "You have enjoyed a walk with your husband this fine afternoon, I hear."

"I have indeed," she said, a smile darting across her lips. "And now I return to hear you teasing our mother mercilessly!"

Amos chuckled as his sister squeezed his arm gently and then went to sit beside their mother, who, much to his relief, was smiling good-naturedly.

"Your brother has always been inclined to such nonsense, has he not?" the Duchess asked, as Flora nodded fervently. "For years, I have near *begged* him to go to London to secure his future, but he has always ignored me!"

"And now, when he says he *will* go, he pretends that you are to warn him from going and seeks instead to pull you back!" Flora added, sounding exasperated whilst, at the very same time, sending him a wink. "How very irritating he is."

"I am able to hear all you are saying of me," Amos interrupted, laughing at the way his mother rolled her eyes. "I apologize for teasing you so, Mother. I know very well that you are very eager indeed for me to make my way into society."

The Duchess smiled back at him, her eyes twinkling. "Indeed I have, for how else are you to find a suitable wife? You must continue on the family line, for you are the Duke of Exeter – and the Duke of Exeter requires an heir!"

"I do have two excellent brothers, however," Amos stated, coming to sit down instead of retreating from the room to leave his mother and sister to talk. "If I cannot find a good wife, then I am certain that they would be very well able to step into the role."

This response brought him nothing but a few minutes

of silence. Amos did his best to keep his expression steady, looking back at his mother with nonchalance while, at the very same time, battling the laughter beginning to burrow into his heart. He knew as well as she did that his two younger brothers – twins, in fact – were quite dreadful when it came to matters of responsibility. They were both still at Eton, being younger than both himself and Flora by some years."

"You are being quite ridiculous now, Amos." The use of his Christian name told Amos that his mother was wearing of his nonsense. "Now, tell me when it is you intend to go to London. This Season, I presume?"

"Within a sennight, I think," Amos told her, choosing now to be quite sensible. "Or mayhap a fortnight, depending on how long it will take for the preparations. Will you wish to come with me?"

His mother's eyebrows lifted. "To London? Oh no, I do not think so."

"No?" This surprised Amos a little. "I thought you might wish to come to London yourself, to return to society and see some of your friends and acquaintances, some of whom you have not seen for a long time."

This made the Duchess shake her head fervently. "I most certainly do not. I am quite contented here at the estate – and I do not want Flora and Galbraith to return to Scotland early, simply because you have determined to leave here and go to London!"

Amos considered this, then nodded. "I understand." His sister and her husband, the Marquess of Galbraith, had come to visit from Scotland and intended to stay for some months. Thus far, they had been with them for a little over two months, but Amos considered, mayhap he was being a little inconsiderate in departing from the estate to London.

"Mayhap I should stay, however. I had not thought about your presence, Flora. I should not want you or your husband to be disappointed at my absence."

"No, no!" Both his mother and sister spoke at once, their eyes wide.

"No, please do not alter your plans for my sake!" his sister continued. "Mother and I will be very contented here at the estate, and you know very well that Galbraith so much enjoys riding and shooting that he will be more than contented until you return. Besides," she continued, a flick of her lips sending a gleam into her eyes, "is it not good that we are here at the very time that you are thinking of finding a bride? It means that we will be present for your wedding day!"

Amos snorted. "You are being a little presumptuous, are you not? I may not find someone suitable this Season. I may have to wait until next Season." The door opened behind him, and he glanced over his shoulder, smiling at his brother-in-law, who immediately came across the room to kiss his wife. "Or mayhap the Season thereafter!"

Flora rolled her eyes at him, then sighed heavily as her husband sat down in the seat beside her. "Must you be so very exasperating? You are a Duke, with a vast fortune and a good deal of land and property. I am certain you will be able to find someone within a week, if you so wish!"

This did not make Amos smile. Instead, it brought a slight weight to his heart, making his brows knot together. "I – I do not think that I would consider a young lady who might only think of my property and fortune."

"That is not what I meant," Flora replied, with a wave of her hand and a look of exasperation. "Come now, *do* be sensible, brother."

"I think he must be considerate all the same." Lord

Galbraith pursed his lips, then shrugged even when his wife shot him a sharp look. "You know as well as I, my dear, that I had to prove myself to your brother *and* to you. I had to show you that I did not care about your standing or your fortune and dowry. I had to prove my heart to you, did I not?" He gestured to Amos but kept looking at Flora. "That will be the same – even more so – for Exeter here. There will be many young ladies desperate for his attention, for they will think only of their potential standing as Duchess!"

This did not bring Amos any encouragement, making him wonder if he should remain at the estate instead of going to London, as he had first thought.

"All the same, there are bound to be *some* young ladies who will not think only of that," Flora said, a hint of desperation in her voice. "You cannot discourage him, Galbraith! You must do all you can to *encourage* him."

Lord Galbraith lifted his shoulders and let them fall for what was now the second time. "I am speaking only as I think right," he said, turning his attention back to Amos. "We are good friends now, are we not? Therefore, I must suggest that you be cautious when you make your way through society. There will not only be young ladies pursuing you but also their mothers, their fathers, aunts and uncles! There will be many of the *ton* who have no interest in you personally but only in the Dukedom and what it might potentially bring them."

"Galbraith, please!" Flora sounded desperate now, perhaps afraid that Amos would refuse to go to London after all. "I cannot think that *any* of this is in any way helpful. I am sure that – "

"He is right." Amos scowled, rubbing one hand over his face before he sat back in his chair with a heavy sigh. "I had not truly thought of such a thing, though I was aware that the *ton* might be a little more... eager in their desire to become acquainted with me, but I did not think seriously about the consequences of that."

There came a short silence in the room, which made Amos' heart twist. His mother, sister, and brother-in-law were all clearly aware that finding a bride who would want to marry him for more than just his fortune and standing might be somewhat difficult, and yet he himself had never really thought of it!

"If you wish, I would be glad to come to London with you."

This made Amos' eyes widen in surprise, just as Flora caught her breath.

"I do not mind returning to society for a time," Lord Galbraith continued, glancing at his wife. "If Flora would prefer me to stay here with her, however, then I would, of course, do so." Smiling, he reached out and took her hand and Flora quickly returned it, showing no upset at such a statement. "Whatever *you* think best, my dear."

Flora looked back at her husband, then turned her gaze to Amos. "It does sound as though you could do with a good friend, Amos."

Amos frowned. "I do have some excellent acquaintances already, Flora. I am sure that they would suffice." Seeing her smile begin to fade, he continued quickly. "Of course, however, I should be very glad to have such fine company, especially given his awareness of my present situation."

"Then it is settled," Flora declared, as smiles began to spread across every face – every face save for Amos. "Galbraith shall go with you to London, and mother and I shall remain here." She turned to the Duchess. "Will that be satisfactory?"

"*More* than satisfactory," their mother said warmly. "I should be very glad to have some time with you alone, my dear."

Amos, who had not said a single word for some minutes, blinked and then cleared his throat. "It seems that all has been arranged for me, then." A little uncertain as to how he felt about such a thing, he could not help but smile at the grin on Lord Galbraith's face. "It seems to me, my friend, that you are quietly delighted about the prospect of returning to London."

"I was not thinking about making my way there until it was suggested, but now – and almost immediately – a great anticipation fills me!" Lord Galbraith admitted. "I have not been amongst society for some time, and there will be many acquaintances there for me to speak with, I am sure. In fact," he continued, getting to his feet, "I think I shall go and begin to make preparations at once. When did you say we were to leave?"

Amos grinned. "Within a sennight," he answered, as Lord Galbraith's shoulders dropped. "I must write to have the townhouse prepared, which I shall do this very afternoon."

"Capital." Lord Galbraith went to sit back down again. "And I am sure that, within a few weeks, we will have found you a suitable bride and you will, very soon, have yourself a very happy and contented situation."

Amos let out a bark of laughter. "I am not certain it will be as simple as that, but I will be very grateful for your company," he said, smiling. "To London we go, then! Let us hope it will be an enjoyable Season, at the very least."

"And let us pray you have success," his mother added emphatically. "For I should like to see you happy and settled here at the estate, Exeter."

About to open his mouth and state that he was already very happy and settled, Amos chose to say nothing and instead, only smiled. His mother had always been furiously determined to see him wed and now, he supposed, she was to get what she wanted... provided he could find the right young lady to marry him!

I do not want someone who thinks only of my wealth or of becoming a Duchess, he thought, setting his jaw tight. *I want to marry someone who knows me as I am, who cares for me and for our future.* His brow furrowed. *I only pray I will be able to find her.*

Chapter Three

Isobella walked arm in arm with Lady Rosalyn through Hyde Park. "It is *such* a fine afternoon, is it not?"

"It is." Lady Rosalyn smiled, then let out a small sigh. "It does feel rather strange having nothing to speak about, does it not?"

"Speak about?" It took Isobella a moment to realize what her friend meant. "You mean that there is no mystery for us to work out, yes?"

Lady Rosalyn chuckled softly. "Yes, that is what I mean. There have been so many things for us to decipher, to uncover and reveal, and now that there is nothing left, I find myself a little... sorrowful, in a way."

"You shall simply have to find some books on the subject," Isobella answered, with a smile. "There are bound to be many things written about mysteries and confusions, I am sure."

"That is true." Lady Rosalyn gave Isobella a sidelong glance. "I am, of course, meant to be thinking on other things, but I confess, there is a part of me that is always eager to learn and to study and to... well, to *think*."

Isobella laughed, squeezing her friend's arm. "That is because you are a bluestocking, is it not? I fully understand what you mean, for I feel the very same way. There is almost an itch within me that cannot be satisfied unless it is scratched by my reading or discussing or, as you have said, *thinking*."

"It is a great pity that so many of the *ton* think poorly of us," Lady Rosalyn murmured, quietly, her smile fading away. "I am grateful that we have found so many friends who *do* accept us, but there is still that weight of disapproval that sits upon us, is there not?"

"There is, yes," Isobella agreed, quietly. "I do not like it, I confess, but I am grateful that my mother and brother do not berate me for it."

"Indeed, that is a blessing." Lady Rosalyn's smile quickly returned. "When I came to London for the Season, I did not ever think that there would be so many gentlemen willing to accept us – though some took a little more convincing than others!"

This made Isobella laugh, recalling how persistent some of her friends had been... and how even in upset and frustration, a love had been borne. "A great deal of convincing in some cases!"

"I do not think you will ever convince me that bluestockings are anything but a blight upon society."

A deep voice interrupted their conversation, and Isobella, a gasp in her throat, spun around to see a tall, thin gentleman with a curled lip narrowing his gaze at them both.

"And you shall never convince me that eavesdropping

upon a conversation is nothing short of impoliteness!" she exclaimed, as Lady Rosalyn's face flushed red. "How dare you speak so? We have not invited you to our conversation, and yet you think it right for you to interrupt us with your thoughts?"

The gentleman sniffed. "I think it is quite acceptable to interrupt *bluestockings,* given that they have such improper views of themselves."

"Improper views?" Lady Rosalyn repeated, her face still flushed. "I do not think I wish to hear what your explanation is in that regard, but I am quite sure you will tell us regardless."

"And that even when we have not been properly introduced!" Isobella added, her heart thumping furiously, though she kept her expression outwardly composed. "That is another sign of your failings in that regard, *sir.*"

The gentleman wrinkled his nose as if to suggest he found their very presence distasteful. "You have no right to question my good standing!"

"If I might step past you, Lord Meadows?" A gentleman that Isobella did not know gave a small smile to the angry, indignant fellow in front of them all. "Forgive me for interrupting your conversation, but the path is a little narrower here."

Lord Meadows' expression brightened at once. "Ah, Your Grace! The very gentleman I needed." He threw out one hand toward Isobella and Lady Rosalyn. "Please, inform these two young ladies that I am of the *greatest* respectability, if you please?"

Isobella's eyebrows lifted, catching the way the Duke's eyes glanced first at her and then at Lady Rosalyn. His expression was one of surprise, though whether it was directed at her or at the question Lord Meadows had put to him, Isobella did not know.

"I – I do not mean to be presumptuous, of course," Lord Meadows stammered, now sounding a little less sure of himself. "Forgive me, Your Grace, you are out walking like the rest of us, and I should not have waylaid you. It is only that *these* young ladies have suggested that I am behaving improperly and I am *greatly* offended."

Lady Rosalyn let out an exclamation of astonishment and Isobella was about to state plainly that Lord Meadows had been the one causing offence in the first place, only for the Duke to frown.

"I do not know what has occurred but I can assure you both that Lord Meadows has always been an upstanding gentleman," he said, his voice quiet but grave. "I am sorry to hear that there has been some accusation of impropriety, however."

Isobella assessed this Duke quickly, a little surprised that he would think to speak so without having asked about the situation in its entirety. He held her gaze steadily, hazel eyes fixing on hers as strands of fair hair brushed across his forehead. There was no anger in his expression, but Isobella could not help but feel upset at his remarks. He had not stopped to ask what Lord Meadows had done to make them respond to him in such a way! That was a little unwise, was it not?

"Yet again, another gentleman has not only approached us but spoken directly to us without being introduced!" Lady Rosalyn turned her head to look at Isobella, but her words were clearly directed at both the gentlemen before her. "I confess, I am greatly astonished at this, especially when one is supposedly a Duke!"

Isobella's lips quirked. "Indeed," she agreed, throwing a look back at Lord Meadows, who was slowly beginning to turn scarlet again. "And for this Duke not to consider what

Lord Meadows might have done to bring us to the conclusion that he was being improper is *also* a little inconsiderate, I think." She smiled lightly at her friend, then let it fall from her face before she turned to look directly at both gentlemen again. Lord Meadows was practically scarlet, but the Duke was frowning, his lips thin. Was he angry with what she had said? Frustrated, mayhap? Isobella told herself she did not much care what he felt, even though there was a slight fluttering of anxiety in her stomach.

The Duke let out a heavy breath, then shook his head. "You are quite correct to say that we have not been introduced. I apologize for that," he said, as Isobella and Lady Rosalyn shared a glance. "Lord Meadows, might you be willing to – "

"Oh, we do not know this gentleman either," Isobella said quickly, looking to Lord Meadows. "He decided that it was his right to not only interrupt our conversation but also to tell us just how disagreeable he found our remarks!"

The Duke blinked, flushed, and then looked to Lord Meadows.

"They are bluestockings!" Lord Meadows began to gesticulate, throwing up both hands and then pointing at Isobella and Lady Rosalyn. "Can you believe that, Your Grace? Bluestockings!"

Isobella lifted her chin, the anxiety in her stomach growing sharply. Just what would this Duke – whose title she did not fully know as yet – say to that?

"I see." The Duke's hazel eyes flashed, his chin lifting a notch. "Bluestockings are certainly – "

"Unwelcome, are they not?" Lord Meadows interrupted, a vein bulging in his temple, his eyes rounded with the anger in his frame. "They think that they can say and do whatever they wish, and those of us in society unfortunate to be in their presence have to simply tolerate it! I most certainly will not, however."

"You have no right to interrupt our conversation, regardless of whether you disagree with our remarks or not," Lady Rosalyn said, loudly enough to speak over anything further Lord Meadows had to say. "And even if you have this Duke to defend you, we shall not change our opinion of your behavior, Lord Meadows. We think you *most* improper, with a dreadful manner and an ill-favored look about you also." She took Isobella's arm again, standing tall as Isobella found herself looking at the Duke, seeing the heavy frown he wore. "I think we shall take our leave now, gentlemen. It would not be *proper* for two young ladies to speak with gentlemen whom they have not been correctly introduced to now, would it?"

Isobella let herself smile coolly before turning away, glad that the conversation had been brought to an end thanks to Lady Rosalyn. Neither gentleman had been particularly agreeable, although the Duke had certainly not done or said anything as upsetting as Lord Meadows.

"Goodness, I am astonished that a gentleman would interrupt us in such a fashion!" Lady Rosalyn exclaimed, walking a little more quickly now. "I think it disgraceful, in fact! How dare he say such things?"

"It was very rude indeed," Isobella agreed, with a glance over her shoulder. The two gentlemen were talking to each other still, with Lord Meadows appearing fairly animated still. "I am surprised that a Duke would speak to us in such a way also, I confess."

"He did apologize at least," Lady Rosalyn said, her voice a bit quieter now. "I am disappointed that he did not challenge Lord Meadows on what he said about bluestockings."

Isobella tried to shrug it off. "Most likely, that is because he agrees," she said, aware that what Lord Meadows had expressed about bluestockings was what the majority of those in society believed. "Come now, let us set that aside and remove it from our minds so we can enjoy the rest of our afternoon."

Lady Rosalyn let out a long breath, set her shoulders, and then smiled. "Yes, you are quite right. We should not let their rudeness upset the rest of our day."

Unable to help herself, Isobella glanced back at the Duke and Lord Meadows again, only to see the Duke looking back at her. Her chest tightened, and she turned her head away quickly, a little embarrassed. "We will forget them both," she said firmly. "I am sure we will have no need to speak to either of them again."

Chapter Four

I must find those two young ladies again.

"Good evening, Your Grace! How wonderful to see you present!"

Amos blinked, then bowed quickly, trying desperately to remember the young lady's name. "Good evening."

"I do hope you are dancing this evening, Your Grace?" The young lady's mother – whose name Amos could not recall either – beamed at him with hope shining in her eyes. "Everyone will be speaking about your presence here this evening and the lucky young ladies that you will stand up with!"

"Alas, I am not to dance this evening," Amos said quickly, seeing the light in the lady's eyes fading. "This is the first ball I have attended this Season, and thus, I have chosen instead simply to greet some old acquaintances and, of course, to make some new ones also."

"Oh." The young lady glanced at her mother, then, glancing up at him from lowered lashes, gave him a coy smile. "Is there no hope of you changing your mind, Your Grace?"

A hand settled on Amos's shoulder. "I am afraid, Lady Gwendoline, that when the Duke of Exeter makes a decision, he is never able to be turned from it. Is that not so, Your Grace?"

Amos glanced at Lord Galbraith as he dropped his hand back to his side, relieved that his brother-in-law had come to his aid. "Indeed it is," he said, looking back at Lady Gwendoline, who now appeared to have tears in her eyes. "Although I am glad to have spoken with you again, Lady Gwendoline. Do excuse me." With another bow and a small smile, he stepped away, with Lord Galbraith beside him. They had only gone a few steps when Amos let out a huff of relief, making Lord Galbraith chuckle.

"Was it truly so very bad?"

"I could not recall her name, *nor* the name of her mother!" Amos exclaimed, pressing one hand to his forehead. "I have been in London for three days now and have met so many new acquaintances, my head is spinning with names and faces! Thank goodness you arrived when you did, for I should be quite without hope otherwise." Lord Galbraith had taken his own carriage from the townhouse to the ball, suggesting that Amos might like to linger for a little longer than he himself. Amos had driven to the ball first and had, upon stepping into the ballroom, been a little overwhelmed by the sheer number of people wishing to speak with him. It had felt as if he were being pressed on every side, being squeezed into a tight box of people. It was not a pleasant experience.

"This is not what I thought it would be," he muttered, aware of how near every eye glanced at him. "I understood that there would be a good deal of attention upon me, certainly, but nothing as severe as this."

Lord Galbraith snorted. "You are a Duke, Exeter. What else did you think would happen?"

Feeling a little embarrassed, Amos looked away, inadvertently catching the eye of a young lady who immediately flushed and batted her eyelashes.

Amos looked away, his stomach twisting. "I presumed that while there would be some attention placed upon me, there would be nothing of this... intensity. Everywhere I go, I have near every young lady or their mother watching me, eager to come speak with me. I am forced to try and remember their names and titles whilst, at the same time, seeking to speak to them in a manner that does not seem rude, especially when they ask me such direct questions!"

"Such as, asking if you are to dance or not?"

"Precisely! What was I meant to say to that?" Amos pushed one hand over his hair, wanting to tug at his collar but choosing not to do so for fear that he would ruin his cravat. "If I said that yes, I was, then she would have the expectation that I would ask her to dance. Which I did not want to do."

Lord Galbraith offered a small, understanding smile. "You are free of it for this evening, so be glad of that. You shall have to dance at the next ball, however, for the *ton* will begin to speak of it if you do not."

Amos scowled. "I do not like society a good deal, I think."

"And yet," his friend said, with a chuckle, "within it, you must find yourself a suitable bride."

I fear I have no hope of that. These first three days had overwhelmed Amos somewhat. There had been so many people near him, all determined to speak with him, to introduce themselves to him, to simply be *near* him! How was he ever to find someone suitable when he could not near breathe without garnering the attention of at least five or six young ladies?

"Do not be so disheartened!" Lord Galbraith said, slapping Amos on the back. "The *ton* will lessen in their attentions towards you very soon, I am sure." He winced. "It will not lessen a great deal, but it *will* lessen somewhat. Come, let us stand over here where the shadows hang a little lower."

This did not bring Amos a good deal of comfort, but the glass of whisky he was handed thereafter, did. Taking a sip, he let out a small sigh and then looked about him.

"Mayhap you will do something dreadful and offend and upset a good many of the *ton*," Lord Galbraith said, with a grin. "That way, you will not have anywhere near the same attention as you have at present."

Amos snorted. "I have already offended two young ladies, I am afraid, but that was entirely accidental. I was a little foolish and much too forward, I will admit, but all the same, I have no intention of doing anything like that again."

"Oh?" Lord Galbraith cocked his head. "What did you do?"

With a roll of his eyes, Amos told him briefly about his encounter with not only Lord Meadows but the two ladies he had been speaking with. "As I said," he finished, "I spoke hastily and without considering what Lord Meadows might have done. I also fear that they believe I feel the same way as he when it comes to bluestockings."

Lord Galbraith scrunched up his face. "I do not have much inclination towards bluestockings, I confess."

"I would never consider a bluestocking, admittedly," Amos agreed, "but I do not think them a stain upon society, as Lord Meadows seemed to suggest."

"And you wish to find them and apologize?"

Amos nodded. "I think it's the right thing for me to do. I do not know their names, however, so that does make it a little more difficult."

"Your Grace! Why are you hiding in the shadows so?"

His stomach knotted but he quickly pushed a smile to his lips. "Good evening, Lord Bristol. And to you also, Miss Shelton." *This* was an acquaintance he remembered, for Miss Shelton was small, dainty but with such a loud voice, he was certain the entirety of the room would be able to hear her the moment she opened her mouth. "Might I introduce you both to the Marquess of Galbraith? He is my brother-in-law, present here with me in London for the Season." Sending the gentleman in question a brief smile, he gestured to the others. "The Viscount of Bristol and his sister, Miss Shelton."

"A pleasure to meet you both." Lord Galbraith swept into a bow.

"A *delight* to meet you," Miss Shelton exclaimed, making Lord Galbraith's eyebrows lift and Amos' lips quirk. "How wonderful it is for you to be present here with the Duke!"

"It is, yes," Lord Galbraith said, casting Amos a wide-eyed glance, forcing Amos to fight the smile that pressed against his lips. "Although I confess that I do miss my wife a good deal."

"Lady Flora, yes?"

Amos turned his head quickly, seeing another two young ladies coming towards him, one with a light smile on her face. His heart sank. Was he not to have even a single moment of conversation with Lord Galbraith? Was his every moment to be interrupted by the arrival of either known or unfamiliar young ladies?

"She is now Lady Galbraith," Lord Galbraith replied, though warmly. "Lady Deborah, yes?"

"Yes, I am." She smiled back at him, ignoring Amos whilst her companion gazed up at him with wide eyes as if she were slightly in awe of him. "I was acquainted with Lady Flora – I mean, Lady Galbraith – for a time."

Which means I ought to recall her also.

"Are you acquainted with the Duke of Exeter, then?" Lord Galbraith asked, as Amos forced a brief smile, seeing Miss Shelton's mouth open and then close again, evidently desperate to say something that would draw his attention back towards her.

"No, I am not." Lady Deborah smiled warmly, her blue eyes looking up at him. "I do not think you were in London at the time of Lady Flora's debut."

That explains why I do not know her. "I was not, no." At that time, his father had still been alive and thus, Flora's debut had been his responsibility. "I would be glad to make your acquaintance, however?"

Lord Galbraith nodded, hastily making the introductions, and Amos smiled, bowed, and did just as he ought to do following a new introduction.

"And then might I present Lady Clara?" Lady Deborah gestured to her friend, who quickly dropped into a curtsy. "Her father is the Earl of Oswestry. Lady Clara, the Duke of Exeter and the Marquess of Galbraith."

"A pleasure," the lady gushed, dipping into what was now her second curtsy. "How glad I am to have met you both. When Lady Deborah told me that she was already acquainted with Lord Galbraith, I was truly delighted!"

Because he is my brother in law and therefore, she can be introduced to me. Amos kept his smile fixed, though his gaze did continually turn towards Lady Deborah. Yes, she had been a little forward in coming to speak with them, but her attention *had* been upon Lord Galbraith for a time, he supposed. And it was her friend who appeared to be so enamored with him! She, Amos considered, was doing very little to catch his attention. That was of note, he had to admit.

"And are you to dance this evening, Your Grace?" Miss Shelton took a step closer to them all, her loud, high-pitched voice capturing the attention of everyone. "We are all so very hopeful that you will be!" She giggled, but the sound grated, making Amos wince. Quickly, he dropped his head and coughed lightly so as to hide the expression from her.

"I have chosen *not* to dance this evening," he said, raising his eyes and seeing her smile crack in an instant. "It is the first ball of the Season for me, and therefore I have chosen to simply be present and converse with as many acquaintances and friends as possible."

"An excellent notion," Lady Deborah said, with a smile of understanding. "I am sure we can all understand that. It must be a little overwhelming to have so many of the *ton* eager for your company!"

This made a wide smile spread across Amos' face. Evidently, this young lady understood exactly what it was he was battling, which Amos had to admit, was very pleasing indeed. "Thank you for your understanding, Lady Deborah," he said, as Miss Shelton opened her mouth to say something more. "I must – oh!" His attention was suddenly caught by a familiar face coming near to him, making his eyes flare and his breath hitch. It was one of the young ladies from the park, when he had spoken a little foolishly and without a great deal of consideration. Someone that he *had* to apologize to.

"Do excuse me," he said hastily, barely glancing at

anyone else present before he stepped away. "I have seen someone I must speak to." Hurrying into the crowd, afraid that the young lady would go out of his sight before he had time to catch her, Amos weaved his way this way and that, never once taking his eyes from the dark copper curls that bounced gently as she walked. Her hair was certainly an unusual color, making it easier for him to keep his gaze trained – and, after only a few more moments, he managed to catch her.

Realizing that he did not know her name, Amos reached out one hand, catching her shoulder for a brief second. "I beg your pardon, but might I have a moment of your time?"

The lady turned her head and looked back at him, her eyes rounding a little. "It would be most improper for me to speak with a gentleman I have not yet been introduced to." One eyebrow arched. "I am also without company at present, for you have waylaid me in following after my brother."

"Then pray, do go after him," Amos said, hastily, "and I will find someone to introduce us. I should very much like to apologize, you understand."

A hint of a smile brushed at her lips, her eyes widening just a fraction. "Is that so?"

He nodded. "It is."

She did not move, did not hurry to rush off after her brother as he might have expected. Instead, she turned to face him a little more, her hazel eyes searching his. Amos said nothing, not certain what it was she was thinking, nor why she lingered as she did. Ought she not to be pursuing her brother, as she had stated?

"I suppose, given the strangeness of our first meeting, we can set aside the formalities." Her lips quirked at his look of surprise. "You did not expect me to say such a thing, I think."

Amos cleared his throat gruffly. "I did not, I confess."

"If you wish for us to find someone to introduce us both, then we can do so, but I fear that may prove a little difficult."

Something about the light lift of her lips settled his heart. "Then I should like to avoid any great difficulty." He bowed low. "I apologize for the awkward manner of our meeting, but I shall introduce myself to you all the same. The Duke of Exeter, my lady."

When Amos lifted his head, the lady was dipping into a low curtsy.

"A pleasure to make your acquaintance, Your Grace," she said, rising to her feet again. "Lady Isobella, daughter to the late Earl of Granville."

The name was not recognizable to him, but Amos smiled all the same. "Thank you, Lady Isobella, for taking the time to speak with me."

Her eyebrow lifted gently. "You were to apologize to me, I think."

Heat rolled into Amos' stomach. "Yes, indeed." With another small inclination of his head, he held her gaze steadily. "I should not have spoken to you and to your companion as I did. I had no knowledge as to what Lord Meadows had said to you and most certainly ought not to have come to his defense without considering first what it was that had caused such upset." He stood tall. "Furthermore, I did not follow the rules of propriety and have us all introduced correctly either. For that, I must apologize."

"An excellent apology, Your Grace."

The heat in Amos' stomach rose into his chest. Was she being facetious or genuinely speaking to him?

"I assume that Lord Meadows informed you about what he said to us?"

Amos shook his head. "He did not. He did, however, state that bluestockings ought to be ignored, that their ideas and notions should be ripped apart and cast aside, so I can imagine that what was said was not in any way complimentary."

"Indeed, it was not." She narrowed her eyes a fraction, studying him. "Might I ask, Your Grace, if his remarks are something you agree with? You need not pretend for my sake, for I should much prefer honesty. It is always good for those of us who *are* bluestockings to know which members of the *ton* would prefer for us not to be in their company."

About to state that he did not think there was anything overly concerning as regarded bluestockings, Amos caught sight of Lord Meadows himself approaching. The gentleman's eyes flared at the sight of Amos speaking with Lady Isobella, but Amos did not make a single move to turn away from her. Having heard Lord Meadows' words on bluestockings, he found himself entirely disinclined towards the gentleman. "I do not have any concerns when it comes to bluestockings," he said, loudly enough for the gentleman to hear. "I do not think they ought to be disregarded, nor do I think that their presence in society should be avoided. If I am to be entirely honest, Lady Isobella, I have not given it a great deal of thought, but, then again, I do not think I need to do so. Bluestockings are a part of society, and I have no intention of turning away from any young lady simply because she determines to be one." Seeing the way Lord Meadows' jaw set, his eyes narrowing and fixing on Lady Isobella, Amos drew himself up, suddenly angry at the fellow for his dislike. "I think that any gentleman who has himself set against bluestockings in such a way ought to be ashamed of himself. He is certainly not a gentleman that I should like to be acquainted with."

Something broke from Lord Meadows' lips, some sort of exclamation but Amos did not return his gaze to the fellow. Instead, he put one hand to his heart and inclined his head. "I hope that will suffice as an explanation, Lady Isobella, and again, I offer you my most sincere apology for my previous mistakes. Please do share my words with your friend also. I will speak to her as well, if she so wishes. My apology is to you both."

Lady Isobella blinked, looking somewhat surprised at his remarks. Then, she smiled, her whole expression softening. "Thank you, Your Grace. You have brought me a good deal of relief, I must admit."

"Then should you like to dance?" Amos asked, completely forgetting about his refusal towards the other young ladies. "It would mean a great deal to me if you would be willing to."

Without a word, Lady Isobella slipped off her dance card and handed it to him. "But of course."

Amos took the dance card quickly, as if he feared it might be snatched back from him if he did not do so. A thrill of delight ran up his spine as he signed his name for the country dance, smiling back at her as he returned the card. "My first dance of the Season," he said, as she slid the ribbon back over her wrist. "Thank you, Lady Isobella. I am looking forward to it."

"As am I," she answered, before bobbing a quick curtsy. "Good evening, Your Grace."

"Good evening." A little surprised at the anticipation that flooded him at the thought of going in search of her and taking her to the dance floor, Amos turned in the direction of Lord Galbraith, a broad smile on his face. Speaking with Lady Isobella had lifted his spirits a good deal, bringing him the first touch of happiness he had found here this evening.

Perhaps being back in society will not be so dreadful after all.

Chapter Five

"**Y**ou danced with the Duke of Exeter, I hear!"

Isobella looked up from the book she was reading. "Good afternoon, brother," she said, snapping her book shut. "Yes, I did."

"What a pity I was not present for it."

"You and Louisa were enjoying a very lovely dinner with Lord and Lady Whitfield, I understand." Isobella gave her brother a broad smile. "Louisa has not yet risen to break her fast, so it must have been an exceptional dinner party!"

This made her brother grin as he came to sit down opposite Isobella. "There were a good many entertainments, I must admit. Louisa is very tired today so I do not think we will see her much before dinner!"

"Will she be joining us for Lord Crawley's ball?"

Lord Granville nodded. "Of course. But you must tell me more about this Duke of Exeter!"

Isobella frowned, not understanding her brother's interest. "I danced with him, that is all. I also danced with the Marquess of Thornbridge, if you care to ask me about him?"

"Ah, you do not know what the *ton* are speaking of this morning, then!" Lord Granville chuckled as Isobella's frown deepened. "You do not know that *you* were the only one he danced with last evening!"

This made Isobella's stomach dip low. "The only one?"

He nodded. "And even worse, he refused the other young ladies who asked if he was to dance, stating that he was choosing not to do so that evening. You can imagine their shock to see him dancing the country dance with you!"

This sent a slight tremor over Isobella's frame, fully aware of what such a thing would mean. The *ton* were already speaking of it, which meant that rumors and gossip might soon be flying through London.

"I did not even know you were acquainted with him!" her brother said, still grinning as if there was something mirthful in all of this. "You did not tell me of your meeting."

"That is because it was not particularly delightful," Isobella answered as her brother's smile dimmed. "He did come to apologize, however, and that is when he asked me to dance."

"Apologize?" Lord Granville looked concerned. "I do hope you are quite all right, Isobella."

"I am." Quickly, Isobella explained all that had happened, seeing him roll his eyes. "I am grateful that you and Louisa do not criticize me for being a bluestocking."

Lord Granville smiled and shrugged. "There is nothing wrong with any young lady seeking to further her knowledge of the world, not as far as I am concerned," he said, firmly. "It does seem as if the Duke of Exeter also feels that way, however." His eyes twinkled as Isobella sighed loudly and looked away. "My dear Isobella, if a Duke is interested in your company, then – "

"He asked me to dance because of his apology and my

acceptance of it, nothing more," Isobella interrupted. "Please, brother, do not see something in the dance that was not there."

"All the same," Lord Granville replied, as the door opened to admit Louisa, "there may be some sort of interest there on *his* part, at least. And you would not refuse a Duke, would you?"

Louisa came to sit down beside her husband, giving Isobella a warm smile. "I think Isobella can refuse whomever she wishes, Granville. If she does not find herself drawn to a Duke, then so be it." When Lord Granville opened his mouth, Louisa pinned him with such a sharp look that he practically withered in front of her, closing his mouth tightly again. Louisa gave Isobella a tiny wink, making Isobella grin at just how much influence the lady had over her husband – and being grateful for it! She had spent many hours talking with Louisa about all that she felt when it came to gentlemen and her hopes of a happy marriage. Louisa knew that Isobella had practically given up any idea of finding a suitable match, that she did not find herself easily able to trust anyone again, and, much to Isobella's relief, Louisa had never once demanded she think otherwise.

"Your dear mother informed me about your dance with the Duke of Exeter," Louisa continued, smiling at Isobella. "I hope he danced well?"

"He did." Isobella considered for a moment, thinking to herself just how easily she and the Duke had been able to converse. "He was very engaging." Her lips drew into a flat line. "He was, of course, nearly surrounded by young ladies and their mothers or fathers once our dance had come to an end." That was certainly one thing that would push her

47

away from a gentleman such as the Duke: the sheer amount of attention his presence would bring.

"That is good. I am glad you had a pleasant evening." Louisa, much to Isobella's relief, drew the conversation to a close. "Now, Granville, did you not say that you would take me to the milliners today?"

Lord Granville's lips flicked upwards. "I am always delighted to step out with you, my love."

"And you will join us, yes?" Louisa looked back at Isobella. "Your mother is on her way out to spend the afternoon with some friends, so we certainly cannot leave you here alone!"

"Mayhap you will have some gentlemen callers and we will be forced to remain at home," Lord Granville suggested, as Isobella rolled her eyes at him. They had been here in London for many weeks now, and she had not, as yet, had any gentlemen coming to call.

"I hardly think so," she said, without complaint nor upset. "Yes, Louisa, I should be very glad to join you."

"But not to the milliners, I think," her sister in law said, with a gleam in her eye. "The bookshop, mayhap? That is where you will want to go, is it not?"

Isobella laughed, glad that Louisa did not mind in the least bit just how much she read. "Yes, quite," she agreed, as her brother nodded his agreement. "Thank you, Louisa. I should like that very much indeed."

The bookshop was not particularly quiet, much to Isobella's frustration. Her maid trailed after her, with both Louisa and Granville still at the milliner's, promising that they would come to the bookshop once their business at the shop was completed. Hopeful that she would find one of her friends present, Isobella made her way directly to the first floor of the bookshop, climbing up the staircase until she emerged into the treasure trove of books. A smile on her face, she looked at each of the shelves, wondering what she might try first. There were so many books here, she was not quite certain where to begin! At the present moment, she was interested in furthering her knowledge of art and artists, for Miss Sherwood was well versed in such a subject and had inspired Isobella in that regard. In addition, she wanted very much to read a little more about the animals not found on England's shores. There were so many, and some sounding so remarkable, they sounded almost fictional! Finally, Isobella thought she might consider reading a novel, something that she could simply sink into and enjoy. With these things in mind, she began to run her fingers along the bookshelves, stopping when she found a book of interest.

"Oh!"

Her heart shot up, a gentleman looming over her. Isobella caught her breath and stumbled back, hitting the bookshelf hard.

"Do excuse me!" the gentleman exclaimed, the book in his hand falling to the floor as he hurried towards her. "I am *dreadfully* sorry, I did not mean to upset you. I was far too caught up with what I was reading and did not even see you."

Isobella rubbed at the small of her back. "I am quite all right," she promised. "Your book, however, is not."

The gentleman turned quickly. With a muttered few words, he went to pick it up and then returned to her, his earnest face filled with apologies yet unspoken.

"I well understand being lost in a book's contents," Isobella said quickly, hoping that he would not linger in conversation, especially when she was here with only her maid. "Please, do not concern yourself."

With a nod, the gentleman took a step back. "I still must heartily apologize," he said, with a small bow. "This is not how I should have liked to introduce myself! The Earl of Preston, ready now to make a full and fervent apology."

Managing to smile, her heart beginning to quieten its thunderous beating, Isobella bobbed a quick curtsy. "Lady Isobella," she said, thinking to herself that this was now the second gentleman she had introduced herself to in what was a less than proper manner. "Please, there is no need for anything further. Might I enquire as to what book garnered your fervent attention?"

Lord Preston smiled, his blue eyes warm, his face a little flushed from the embarrassment of what he had done. "It is a study on birds," he said, looking away from her. "Not something that many a person will enjoy, I am sure, but I find it quite fascinating."

It was not a subject that instantly grabbed Isobella's attention but all the same, she found *his* interest delightful. "I was thinking to myself that I should very much like to learn a little more about some of the animals that have been discovered on the continent," she told him, catching the way her maid came to stand a little closer, albeit with her head lowered and hands clasped in front of her. "I do not know much about birds at all, however."

This sent light spiraling into Lord Preston's eyes. "I should be very glad to speak with you on the subject if you would like?" he asked, making Isobella's lips curve. "I confess, I do speak a little too much at times; however, so you shall have to tell me to be quiet if I go on for far too long."

Considering this quickly, Isobella let her smile grow. "That would be most enjoyable, Lord Preston. Thank you."

"Then I shall arrange to come to call some afternoon, mayhap?" He sounded hopeful, and Isobella nodded. "Wonderful. I shall take my leave now, though I should very much like to begin our conversation now." Glancing about him and, no doubt, seeing the other patrons in the shop, he sighed and shook his head. "Best not to do so, I think, else we shall be standing here for the rest of the afternoon!" He inclined his head. "Good afternoon."

"Good afternoon, Lord Preston," Isobella answered, watching him as he walked away, a little surprised at how happy the conversation had made her. Lord Preston had been an unexpected arrival to her time here in the bookshop, but after their conversation, certainly not an unwelcome one!

But I have no intention of letting my heart follow after him.

That made a frown pull at her forehead, realizing just how easily she might find herself interested in a gentleman's attentions. Had she not learned from her previous mistakes? Had she not been shown just how little she could trust what a gentleman said? First, Lord Brookmire had hoped to court her, only to then step away when she had not been as eager in her attentions as he. Secondly, Lord Pollock had pursued her with such a great and fervent intent, she had believed him wholeheartedly in love with her – until he had disappeared from society one day. She had been distraught, wondering what had happened to him, only to hear that he had eloped with a young lady. Lastly, Lord Hogarth had broken her heart entirely, for she had begun to fall in love with him. His words of love and affection had been nothing but lies, his promises of devotion and adoration crumbling to nothing. Recovering from such a dark situation had been a hard path to walk, but she had done so. With that, however, had come the determination that she would never again let herself be hurt in such a way again – and that meant never permitting herself to have even the smallest interest in a gentleman.

"And I shall not," she stated aloud, her maid looking up in surprise. "I will never again let myself fall in love again."

Chapter Six

Amos put his hands behind his back and tried to smile. "Why yes, I did only dance once at the ball," he said, seeing Lady Deborah frown. "But there was a good reason for that."

"Oh?" Lady Clara lifted one eyebrow, her lips pursed and what looked like a glint of anger in her eyes. "Why would you stand up with a *bluestocking* and not with the likes of us?"

A little taken aback by the lady's irritation, Amos wondered if he ought to frown and remind the lady that she had no right to question him as she was doing, only to set that idea aside. It would only cause her a little more upset, he considered, if he were to do such a thing. "It was by way of apology," he explained, choosing not to say anything more on the subject. "But I have promised you all that I shall dance this evening, have I not?"

This made Lady Clara scowl instead of smile, as Amos had hoped. "You will have an excuse again, I fear."

"Clara!" Lady Deborah turned to her friend, putting a

hand on her arm. "We must trust the Duke's word. If he had good reason to stand up with Lady Isobella, then we must accept it... *and* look forward to the dance this evening." Her light smile was quickly directed back towards him. "I am sure that the Duke will do as he has said."

"I most certainly shall," Amos determined, although inwardly frustrated that he was going to have to dance with Lady Clara and, no doubt, Miss Shelton when she discovered that he was to dance.

"I hope you do not mind if I join this conversation?"

Amos glanced to his right as a gentleman he was not yet acquainted with came to join them. He was a heavy-set fellow, with eyebrows sitting low over his eyes with his jaw jutting forward. This gave him the appearance of being most displeased with something although Amos considered that might well just be his own perception.

"Lord Welton, of course." It was Lady Clara who spoke first, putting a smile on her face and then gesturing to Amos. "Might I introduce you to the Duke of Exeter? Your Grace, this is the Earl of Welton."

Amos bowed. "Glad to make your acquaintance."

The gentleman returned the bow but said nothing, no smile on his face.

"What was it you were all discussing?" he asked, turning his attention now to Lady Deborah. "Something of importance, no doubt!"

Lady Clara laughed at this, making Amos squirm inwardly. "Oh, not at all. We were only asking the Duke of Exeter why he stood up with a young lady at the ball when he had told both me *and* Lady Deborah that he was not to dance at all! He has promised to dance with us at the ball this evening; however, we have decided to forgive him."

Lord Welton snorted. "Not of importance in the least,

then!" He threw a look towards Amos. "Yes, I did hear about some Duke or other dancing with a bluestocking. A most extraordinary choice of partner, Your Grace, especially when you have such ladies as Lady Deborah and Lady Clara beside you!"

Disliking this particular remark, Amos let the edge of his lip curl but said nothing more, not at all interested in hearing anything further about Lady Isobella.

"You must think poorly of bluestockings, Your Grace," Lord Welton continued, nudging Amos with his elbow in a most displeasing manner. "Most gentlemen in London think that way about them! There can be nothing good about such creatures, I am sure."

"I do not think the same way, then," Amos replied, snapping his heels together. "I shall take my leave of you all now and permit Lord Welton to have a conversation with you both in peace. Good afternoon."

"Oh, Your Grace, please!"

Much to Amos' surprise, Lady Clara stepped forward just as he was turning. Her hand reached out, grabbing at him, clearly determined to pull him back, only for her hand to snag on one of the buttons of his tailcoat. There came a pop, and, with that, the sound of something tearing. Lady Clara let out a squeak of surprise, then put both hands to her cheeks, her face now scarlet.

Amos looked down, seeing not only one button half torn from his tailcoat but another quite gone, leaving a hole where it ought to be. Every eye would be on him now, he was sure, for he could not easily walk through Hyde Park at the fashionable hour without being seen and this discrepancy noted!

"I can only apologize," Lady Clara whispered, tears shimmering in her eyes as Amos glanced at her and then stepped back, looking all around for the missing button. "I only meant to catch your arm for a moment."

Seeing the button, Amos bent to pick it up. "Of course." Struggling to smile against his own sense of embarrassment and the beginnings of anger, he bowed sharply. "Pray, think nothing of it. Do excuse me."

As he began to walk away, he heard Lady Clara begin to cry, but did not turn his head to step back towards her. There was no comfort he could offer, not at this present moment. Quite what she had been doing, Amos could not imagine, for it was most improper for any young lady to grasp at his arm in the way she had done! This had not been a very pleasant afternoon, he considered, for the conversation with Lady Deborah and Lady Clara had not been enjoyable, and the arrival of Lord Welton had added nothing to it either! He had heard more than one person present remarking upon his single dance – and with a bluestocking no less – and now, no doubt, there would come more whispers about the state of his tailcoat!

All the same, I do not regret dancing with her, he thought to himself, striding across the park and doing his best to avoid looking at any of the other ladies and gentlemen who tried to catch his gaze. *Lady Isobella was very lovely indeed.*

He stopped suddenly, his brow furrowing. Lady Isobella was not someone who had appeared in the least bit taken with his standing as a Duke. She had spoken to him quite sharply at times, had shown no deference, and had not once attempted to be coy or teasing. Neither had she hidden the fact that she was a bluestocking from him, which was all the more noteworthy! If she had wanted to catch his attention in any way, then might she not have pretended she was *not* such a thing?

"She is beautiful, intelligent, and without façade," he murmured aloud, his heart beginning to quicken its pace. "Might I not think of pursuing *her*?"

It was a strange thought, an unexpected one, but the more Amos let himself think on it, the more certain he became. Was this not what he had wanted? Had he not told himself that he wanted a young lady who would not gaze up at him with shining eyes, lost in a dream of good fortune and high standing? A smile began to spread across his face, his hope rising sharply. If he called upon her, then surely within a week or two, he would know for certain whether or not she was someone he could be drawn to! He would learn more about her, see more of her character, understand her all the better – and from that, could not courtship be in view?

His reverie was suddenly shattered by the loud crack of lightning, making him jump in fright. The thunder that came thereafter sent a tremor through his bones, swiftly followed by the beginnings of what swiftly became a downpour. All around him, gentlemen and ladies began to scramble for their carriages, with some screaming with fright at the furious sounds. Amos began to hurry, his ruined tailcoat now catching the brunt of the rain. He had quite forgotten where his carriage was, losing his bearings all the more in the melee that quickly swallowed him up. Relentless, the thunderstorm drove everyone from the park, soaking many – including Amos – to the bone.

Amos shoved one hand through his hair, grimacing. "No, Galbraith. I did not have the very best of afternoons."

His brother-in-law chuckled, tipping his head as he regarded Amos. "I can see that."

"The fashionable hour was... " Taking a hold of his coat with each hand, he pulled it back a little, seeing the drips of water collecting at the edges. "It was a disaster."

Lord Galbraith's smile did not fade. "I presume that you had many a conversation, however? *Before* the rain, I mean?"

Amos stripped off his tailcoat and began to unbutton his waistcoat. He would take both to his bedchamber in a moment, where the valet could do his best to salvage them. "I had some. Most of them involved people demanding to know why I stood up with a bluestocking and refused to dance with any other." He scowled, holding up the ripped tailcoat. "*This* was Lady Clara's attempt to keep me in her company when I tried to move away." Grimacing, he shook his head. "The arrival of a Lord Welton pushed me from that conversation, but it appears she was determined to have me stay!"

"Goodness." The smile on Lord Galbraith's face was gone now. "That is a little... unfortunate."

"I shall have it replaced, if it cannot be repaired," Amos shrugged, "but it is the audacity of her actions which troubles me! Lady Deborah is not at all the same as her friend, but all the same, she *did* seem upset that I stood up with Lady Isobella and not with her."

"Understandably."

This gave Amos pause.

"You said to three ladies, if not more, that you were not to dance," Lord Galbraith said, as Amos pushed his fingers through his wet hair for the second time. "Then you forgot yourself and danced with Lady Isobella. They feel slighted, which is something I can understand."

Amos grimaced. "It was not intentional."

"I know." Lord Galbraith sighed and then sat back in his

chair, eyeing Amos. "But you are the Duke of Exeter. As I have said to you, time and again, you are going to be pursued by nearly every eligible young lady here in London!" He eyed Amos's tailcoat. "I did not think that it would ever reach such an extent that your clothes would be torn, but all the same, that is something you must expect! Every young lady who is eligible will want to catch your eye."

"Except for the bluestocking herself."

Lord Galbraith's eyebrows shot upwards.

"Lady Isobella, I mean," Amos continued, walking across to where the decanter of whisky sat at the opposite end of the drawing room. "As I was walking away from Lady Clara and Lady Deborah, I realized that Lady Isobella was quite different from them both."

"Oh? In what way?"

Amos poured a measure for himself and then one for Lord Galbraith. "She did nothing to garner my attention. Nor did she seek me out, eager for me to notice her." Handing one glass to Lord Galbraith, he took a small sip of his own whisky, smacking his lips together as the heat began to wash over him. "I realized that young ladies want to do whatever they can to catch my interest. If I were she, I would not say anything about being a bluestocking, knowing what society thinks of them."

"And yet, she did," Lord Galbraith said, speaking slowly as Amos nodded fervently. "She has told you from the beginning that she is a bluestocking."

"Even when she knew I was a Duke, she did not even think to hide that about herself," Amos continued, warming to the subject. "The way she has spoken to me is unlike any other young lady I have met as yet. There is frankness there, a direct manner of speaking that is both refreshing and surprising."

Lord Galbraith began to smile. "Does this mean that you are thinking of considering her as a bride?"

Scoffing at this, Amos sat down in a chair, only to get up again as the dampness of his clothes stuck to his skin. "Not as a bride, no, not as yet. I do not know her well enough yet to consider such a thing."

"Then you will call upon her, I presume?"

Nodding, Amos' heart lifted with a fresh hope. "Yes, I think I shall. Take tea, and the like."

"You are aware that the *ton* will speak of such a thing, yes?"

That made Amos frown, his hopes crumbling at the edges. "I confess, I had not thought of that."

"Then mayhap do not call upon her," his brother-in-law suggested. "Not as yet. You might, instead, walk through the park at the same time as she and unexpectedly meet."

Amos chuckled. "A little more clandestine, yes?"

"Yes, but it is to keep the gossip from you both. Until, mayhap, you decide whether or not to pursue a connection with her."

"An excellent notion." Throwing back the rest of his whisky, Amos let out a sigh of contentment. "You have greatly improved my afternoon, Galbraith. I thank you. Now, however, I must go and change."

"And see if your tailcoat can be repaired," Lord Galbraith called after him, as Amos quit the room. "Perhaps the buttons need to be sewn on with double the amount of thread so that Lady Clara will not be able to pull them from you again!"

Laughing, Amos walked out of the room and made his way towards his bed chamber, more than ready for this afternoon to be at an end. The ball this evening should be an excellent one, and with any luck, he might find Lady Isobella again. Yes, he would have to dance with all those he had promised to already, but mayhap he would also be able to stand up with her, and that, Amos considered, would be a very enjoyable time indeed.

Chapter Seven

"**Y**ou do not look as though you are enjoying this ball in any way."

Isobella glanced at her friend. "Oh, but I am," she said, not wanting Lady Amelia to think her bored or dulled. "It is a very pleasant evening thus far."

Lady Amelia sighed. "Ah, but we are all a little more... fragmented, are we not?" she said, softly. "We have all found ourselves a suitable gentleman, and you are left alone. We should be considering you a little more, I am sure, and – "

"You are doing nothing wrong," Isobella replied, interrupting her friend gently. "Please, do not trouble yourself on my account. I am quite contented."

"But shall you be in the future?" Lady Amelia wanted to know, giving Isobella a searching look. "Will you truly be happy alone?"

Recalling how she had previously expressed to Lady Amelia that she had no need for an attachment, Isobella shrugged lightly. "I am determined to be happy."

Lady Amelia's lips twisted to one side.

"I have already had a time of being in love," Isobella continued, feeling the weight of the memories beginning to pull down her heart. "I do not need to be so again."

"Why ever not?" Lady Amelia's eyes were wide as they made their way to the side of the ballroom, stepping out of the large crowd and into a quieter part of the ballroom. "Why would you step back from it if it was offered to you again?"

Isobella hesitated. She had not spoken of her past with very many people at all, and certainly none of her friends knew of her pain. In attempting to keep it out of her heart and mind, in trying to step away from the pain and to leave it in the past, Isobella had determined to say nothing to anyone, and yet, now there came a tug of longing to share with her friend all that had transpired.

"You do not need to tell me if you do not wish to." Lady Amelia ducked her head, looking a little embarrassed. "I will not be in the least bit upset if you choose to keep it to yourself; I ought not to be pressing you."

"It is all right." With a small sigh, Isobella closed her eyes. "I have not shared this with anyone, Amelia. Mayhap I should have done, but I thought to try and forget about it."

Lady Amelia said nothing, and Isobella, swallowing at a lump in her throat, tried to explain.

"I have had three gentlemen interested in pursuing me," she said, as Lady Amelia's eyes rounded. "The first was very eager, but as I was considering his request for courtship, he decided that I was taking much too long and stepped away."

This made Lady Amelia's brow furrow almost immediately. "That says nothing good about his character."

Isobella smiled ruefully. "I suppose that is true. Lord Pollock came next, and he was quite determined to pursue me." Her head lowered, her gaze on the floor as shame began to climb up through her. "I thought him quite wonderful, truth be told. He was devoted, it seemed."

"But he did not prove himself to be as you expected?"

With a nod, Isobella glanced at her friend, feeling fire in her cheeks. "He eloped. Most unexpectedly."

With a gasp, Lady Amelia stared back at Isobella, her hand going to her arm. "You mean to say you had no knowledge of another attachment?"

She shook her head.

"That is utterly disgraceful," Lady Amelia declared, tossing her head. "How dare he do such a thing? What a dreadful gentleman!"

With a smile at her friend's solidarity, Isobella took in another breath and then continued. This was the most painful part. "I was determined to be more careful during my second Season," she said, looking away, surprised that there were tears burning in her eyes. "I thought that Lord Hogarth was truly in love with me. He was different from Lord Brookmire and Lord Pollock. There was a genuineness to all his words, his determination to be by my side so sincere, I could not help but believe him. I – I do not like to admit this, but I did fall in love with him." She wiped at her eyes. "There came a time when I recognized that I felt more for him than I had felt for any other. My feelings were not overly severe, I admit, but they were certainly present."

"And then he broke your heart completely and utterly," Lady Amelia said quietly. "Is that not so?"

With a deep breath, one that seemed to pull her very heart a little further up into her chest, Isobella nodded. "Yes, he did." A single tear fell to her cheek, but she dashed it away. "He told me that he did not care for me any longer. I could not understand him, could not comprehend why he would say such a thing, only to discover that he had not been as devoted to me as he had promised." Her eyes closed tightly, the urge to keep this last part from her friend very strong indeed. She spoke it all the same. It *needed* to be said. "My brother found a bet in Whites betting book that involved Lord Hogarth and a particular widow. The bet had been fulfilled."

"Oh, Isobella." Lady Amelia embraced her at once, her sympathy and compassion comforting Isobella a little. "I cannot imagine the pain that you have endured."

"It was very difficult," Isobella admitted, her voice wobbling as she tried to regain her composure. "I did not know what to do nor what to say when he first told me that the engagement was broken. The *ton* knew of it all very soon thereafter, of course, and whilst they spoke ill of him, as they ought, there were still remarks made about me."

"Something there should not have been," Lady Amelia said, a heavy line drawing between her eyebrows. "You do not trust any gentlemen now, then?"

Isobella nodded. "Precisely."

"And so you have determined to be alone? You will become a spinster?"

Relieved that her friend understood, Isobella spread out her hands. "My mother, brother, and sister in law are all determined that I *shall* find someone this Season, although they do not push me with any force into it for which I am grateful."

Lady Amelia tilted her head, watching Isobella carefully. "But you have determined to remain alone."

"Yes."

"And what if," Lady Amelia asked, still frowning, "a suitable gentleman does begin to pursue you? What then?"

Isobella's lips quirked. "I hardly think that will happen. I am a little older than you all and, besides that, I am a bluestocking. It is not as if gentlemen in London will be pursuing ladies such as myself!"

"And why should they not?" Lady Amelia exclaimed, her voice suddenly louder than before. "You think too low of yourself, Isobella."

Caught off guard by her friend's vehemence, Isobella blinked and pressed her lips together, feeling the urge to defend her position and yet, at the same time, understanding her friend's sharp remarks.

"Has there not been whispers about you these last few days, ever since that Duke stood up with you – and *only* you at the ball?"

"That means nothing," Isobella said, quickly. "Come now, you must see that his request was only because of the apology he had made and his desire to make certain all was well between us."

Lady Amelia arched her eyebrow. "And what if it was not? What if there was more to his desire to dance with you than you were aware?"

"No." Isobella shook her head fervently, fear tightening her core. Fear that if she let herself even *think* such a way, it would do nothing but cause her yet more agony. "No, Amelia, I do not believe that for a moment. Even if it were a possibility, I would not think to consider it, for I cannot let my heart free again." She took another deep breath and then pushed back her shoulders. "It is certainly *not* a possibility, however. I am quite sure that the Duke of Exeter will never again seek me out to dance."

"Lady Isobella?"

The moment she finished saying those words, a voice broke into their conversation and, turning, Isobella snatched in a breath of surprise.

"It *is* you," the Duke said, his warm smile spreading

across his face. "How good to see you again." Seeing Lady Amelia, he inclined his head towards her. "Might you introduce me to your companion?"

Ignoring the knowing smile on Lady Amelia's face, Isobella quickly made the introductions, desperately hoping that the Duke had not heard her speaking of him. "Of course. Lady Amelia, this is the Duke of Exeter." She waited as Lady Amelia dipped into a curtsy. "Your Grace, might I present my dear friend, Lady Amelia."

"I am very glad to make your acquaintance," he said, bowing again. "I have come in the hope that you might both offer me your dance cards? I have determined to dance again this evening, you see."

Isobella blinked in surprise, for everything she had just said and thought was now ripped up and thrown aside at the Duke's words. He had, despite her belief he would not, come to see if she *would* dance after all! This time, at least, it was not only her who would be standing up with him, although Isobella was sure the *ton* would still take note of her standing up with him again.

"How very kind of you, Your Grace. I should be delighted." Lady Amelia slipped off her dance card and handed it to him, throwing a wide-eyed look towards Isobella. She swallowed hard, aware that she could not easily refuse and, after a moment, handed her dance card to the Duke.

"Wonderful!" The Duke smiled broadly as he took the dance card from her and, as he did so, their eyes meeting, Isobella's stomach began to swirl with a gentle, soft warmth. A warmth that she had felt before, albeit some years ago. The Duke was handsome, of course, but it was the kindness of his smile and his sincerity that began to tug at her heart.

And I cannot let it.

"I must hope that you will let me sign your dance card thereafter, Lady Isobella?"

Astonished at the arrival of yet another gentleman, Isobella's eyes rounded as Lord Preston came to stand beside them, his gaze going to Lady Amelia. "Lord... Lord Preston," she said, a little overwhelmed by not one but two gentlemen now seeking to dance with her. "Are you acquainted with Lady Amelia?"

"I am, in fact," he said, as Lady Amelia smiled at him. "I am acquainted with Lord Broughton who has given me the great pleasure of being introduced to his betrothed."

"A good evening to you, Lord Preston," Lady Amelia said, with a smile. "A pleasure to see you again."

"I hope you are dancing also, Lady Amelia?" Lord Preston asked, as the Duke returned the card to Isobella, no smile on his face now as his gaze flicked towards Lord Preston. "I should be very pleased to stand up with you both."

Isobella glanced at the Duke, then back to Lord Preston. "Might I ask if you are both already acquainted?"

Lord Preston smiled and then nodded at the Duke. "Yes, we are, although it was many years ago when we first made our acquaintance!"

The Duke blinked and frowned, only for his eyes to flare. "In Eton, I think."

"Yes, precisely!" Lord Preston grinned, then took his gaze to the dance card. "Many years ago now. It is good to see you again, Your Grace."

"And you also," came the reply, but there was no easy smile to accompany those words. "I shall take my leave now and leave you to your conversation." He smiled quickly in Isobella's direction. "I look forward to our dance, of course."

She smiled back at him, then took the dance card from

Lord Preston's fingers, searching for where both gentlemen had chosen to sign their names. Lord Preston had taken the cotillion, but to her utter astonishment, the Duke of Exeter had chosen to take the waltz. Her stomach dipped, her breathing quickening as Lady Amelia and Lord Preston continued a conversation around her. Why had he taken the waltz? Had he no understanding that the *ton* would speak all the more of a connection between herself and the Duke, one that was not there? Or was it that he simply did not care?

There cannot be any real interest there, she told herself, firmly. *And if there is, I cannot let myself respond to it. I can never trust him, I can never again let my heart be free... not even if the gentleman in question is a Duke.*

Chapter Eight

Amos glanced around the room, taking in everyone present in the drawing room, at least. His lips twisted in frustration. As yet, he could not spy Lady Isobella, and he had been very much hoping she would be present.

"She is not here, then?"

Glancing at Lord Galbraith, Amos shrugged. "I thought she might be, so I could continue my study of her, but alas, I fear not."

Lord Galbraith grinned at him, his eyes twinkling. "You are pursuing the lady with a great deal of intensity, my friend – and that even without courtship!"

Again, Amos shrugged. "I must. If I am to find an appropriate young lady, then I must do all I can to find out whether someone I am considering could be suitable – and that *before* I suggest courtship. As you yourself have said, I do not want to have the *ton* whisper about me or the lady in question before it is decided how one should proceed."

"Indeed, you are very wise," his friend agreed, albeit

with a gleam still lingering in his eyes. "The *ton* still speak of you all the same, however."

Amos grimaced. "I am sure they do, and I am all the more certain that they shall continue to do so regardless."

"And you are still interested in Lady Isobella?"

He nodded. "Yes. We danced at Lord Murton's ball some two days ago now, and we did manage to have a short conversation thereafter. She introduced me to her brother who suggested I might like to come to call one afternoon – much to Lady Isobella's embarrassment, I might add." Chuckling at the memory of Lady Isobella's face beginning to turn a deep scarlet, he reached out to take a glass of brandy from the passing footman. "I am determined to spend a little more time in her company before I decide whether to do such a thing or not. I do not want to add to her own embarrassment for I am sure that the *ton*'s whispers have affected her also."

Lord Galbraith snorted. "I do not think she will be in the least bit concerned about that."

"No?"

"Any young lady would be glad to have whispers spoken about herself and a Duke, I am sure!" With a sip of his brandy, Lord Galbraith spread out his other hand, gesturing to all the young ladies in the room. "They all require a good match, do they not? What better match than a Duke! If society begins to push a young lady and a gentleman of high standing together by their gossip, then what trouble does that bring to her? It can only be a good thing."

Hoping that Lord Galbraith was right, Amos set aside any concern he had over Lady Isobella. "Do you recall Lord Preston? He was also eager to dance with Lady Isobella."

"Lord Preston?" Lord Galbraith frowned, only for his

eyes to flare. "Yes, I do recall him. A little bookish, was he not?"

A dull thud kicked in Amos' stomach. "Yes, he was." *A perfect match for a bluestocking.* "He studied much more fervently at Eton than I did, I will admit."

"And you say that he was interested in dancing with her also?" Lord Galbraith asked, as Amos nodded. "I see." His smile lifted the edges of his lips again. "Then let us hope that you do not have any competition when it comes to the lady!"

Amos was about to open his mouth and state he was sure he had nothing to worry about – even when his mind was a little troubled over that very thing – only for Lady Deborah to come towards them both. She was smiling lightly, perhaps contented with him now that he had danced with her as he had promised.

"Good evening, Lord Galbraith, Your Grace." Bobbing a quick curtsy, she glanced behind her. "I wanted to introduce you to another acquaintance of mine, Lady Victoria. She is the cousin of Lord Welton, you see. Alas, she is busy in conversation with another of our friends." Turning back, she smiled at Amos. "I am sure she will join us very soon."

Amos nodded. "I am always glad to make new acquaintances." Lady Deborah was certainly someone he would be willing still to consider, he thought to himself, although she did not bring up the same interest as he had with Lady Isobella. Lady Deborah was amiable with excellent conversation without being in the least bit demanding of him, but she did not have the same spark as Lady Isobella did.

Am I truly that drawn to Lady Isobella? Amos wondered to himself as Lord Galbraith and Lady Deborah began to speak on the most recent ball. *So much so that I would consider her first above any other?*

"You are going to dance again this evening, I hope?"

"This evening?" Amos repeated, pulled out of his thoughts as Lady Deborah nodded. "I did not know there was to be dancing."

Lady Deborah smiled at him. "It seems our host has decided that it would be an excellent thing to end the soiree with," she said, as another young lady – willowy, with piercing blue eyes and a gentle smile – came towards them. "You will be much in demand, Your Grace. Mayhap I should have you promise one dance to me at this very moment so you are not overrun with demands before I can reach you!"

This was said with a small, somewhat coy smile, and Amos, rather than delighting in it, fought hard not to frown. Lady Deborah did not have any claim upon him, and he certainly did not want her to think that he was willing to consider her before any other.

"Forgive my tardiness, Lady Deborah." The young lady, as yet unintroduced came to stand beside her friend. "Might you make the introductions?"

"But of course."

Within a few minutes, Amos and Lord Galbraith became acquainted with Lady Victoria whose sharp eyes unsettled Amos somewhat. No doubt she would be considered beautiful, but there was something about her expression that Amos did not quite like. Perhaps it was the watchful way she fixed her gaze on him or the cool, quiet way she spoke. Whatever it was, Amos was not in the least bit drawn to her.

"You were arranging to dance before I interrupted," Lady Victoria said, once the introductions were made. "Forgive me for that. Please, do continue."

Amos swallowed thickly, seeing the way Lady Deborah's eyes flashed with expectation. "Alas, I have chosen not to dance this evening," he said, as Lady Deborah's smile slid to the floor. "I do not think I should like to do so."

"It is just as well there are so many *other* gentlemen for you to dance with, then," Lady Victoria murmured, speaking directly to Lady Deborah rather than to Amos. "Come now, you need not look so disappointed."

"I am not at all disappointed," Lady Deborah remarked briskly, her tight, thin-lipped smile betraying her. "Are you often so unwilling to dance, Your Grace? I thought eligible gentlemen of the *ton* could hardly wait to dance with the young ladies of London!"

Casting a quick look towards Lord Galbraith, Amos lifted his shoulders and then let them fall. "I am a little fatigued, that is all." He did not give her any further explanation than that, thinking to himself that Lady Deborah did not require it from him. "There are always so many opportunities for dancing, are there not? I am sure we will be able to stand up together very soon."

"Indeed." Lady Deborah sniffed, lifted her chin, and slid him a slightly subversive look. "Do excuse us, Your Grace, Lord Galbraith."

Amos watched them leave, a heaviness settling on his shoulders, pushing him down into the floor. "It seems like no matter what I do or say, I am bound to offend someone in some way."

"You refused to dance with her again," Lord Galbraith said, with a chuckle. "I am afraid you have disappointed her, but there is nothing wrong with that, especially if you are not to pursue her."

"I am not, not as yet," Amos muttered, watching the ladies depart from him, their backs straight and shoulders pulled back. "I did not ever think that traversing society would be this difficult!"

"That is precisely why I am here, is it not?" Lord Galbraith grinned at him, making Amos smile despite his frustrations. "I am able to guide and direct... and to keep you encouraged." His smile lingered. "And with that in mind, I should say that I think Lady Isobella a very good consideration."

"What do you know of her?"

Lord Galbraith laughed at the question, perhaps seeing the sharpness in Amos' eyes. "I have done a *little* investigating, I have to admit. It is my duty, is it not? If she is someone that you are to consider seriously, then I felt it right for me to learn what I could about her."

Amos snorted. "You are my chaperone, then?"

"Something like that – though Lady Isobella has nothing displeasing about her, much to my relief."

Amos blinked. "No?"

"No, not in the least. She is a little older than some of the debutantes and the other young ladies; she was absent from society last Season, but there is nothing about her character that I can see as being displeasing." He shrugged. "There was one whisper or two about a particular gentleman ending their engagement, but I learned that was because of his poor behavior and had nothing whatsoever to do with her."

It was as if the room had filled with light, pushing away his frustration and upset over Lady Deborah's behavior. It was as if it confirmed to him that yes, Lady Isobella *was* the one he ought to be considering. Taking a sip from his glass, he let out a small, contented sigh. "That is good news."

"You have my blessing," Lord Gainsworth told him, in a fatherly manner, laughter burning in his eyes at the roll of his eyes that Amos sent him. "Let us hope she will consider you else you will be quite without hope!"

Amos laughed ruefully. "That would be quite disconcerting, certainly." He took in a breath, setting his shoulders back. "Let us hope it does not come to that."

"Lady Isobella! Lady Rosalyn. Is this not a pleasant afternoon?" The smile that spread across Amos' was genuine, thrilled to see both the ladies in question.

"Good afternoon, Your Grace." Lady Rosalyn bobbed a curtsy, as did Lady Isobella. "Yes, it is a very pleasant day. The sun is not too hot and whilst there are clouds, I do not think it will rain." She exchanged a smile with her friend. "That downpour last week was quite extraordinary!"

"I was caught in it, unfortunately," he told them, though neither of them looked at all horrified but did their best to hide their smiles. "I was quite drenched!" He laughed and shook his head at the memory. "Lord Galbraith – my brother-in-law – found it quite mirthful. I am sure I looked quite ridiculous!"

This made both the ladies giggle, and Amos smiled back at them, looking into Lady Isobella's eyes and thinking to himself just how much they lightened whenever she smiled. With her copper curls and hazel eyes, she had a beauty all of her own, and Amos could not help but be drawn to her.

"I must also make certain to apologize to you for the first time we met in this park, Lady Rosalyn," he continued, before anything more could be said. "I know that I have apologized to Lady Isobella and did ask her to pass it on to you also, but I think it right that I tell you in person just how sorry I am for not only jumping to conclusions but also speaking to you in the manner I did."

Lady Rosalyn smiled at him. "There is no need for further apology, Your Grace," she assured him. "I thank you for it, however."

He nodded, then glanced at Lady Isobella. After the conversation with Lord Galbraith last evening, he found himself all the more certain that this was the lady he wanted to begin to pursue. "Might I walk with you for a time?"

"I must excuse myself." Lady Rosalyn gave no reason for this and clearly did not notice Lady Isobella's instantly flared eyes, giving him a nod of her head. "Lady Isobella's sister in law, Lady Granville, is just over there." She directed him to where two ladies sat on a bench near them, deep in conversation. "So long as you are not too far from her, I am sure all will be well. I will tell Lady Granville that you are walking with Lady Isobella, so they know where she is gone."

"I thank you." Sensing that the lady had a purpose in her absence, Amos gave her a broad smile, silently thanking her for her absence. "Lady Isobella, should you like to follow this path? I can see that it leads around the park in a small circle, and we will not go out of sight of Lady Granville."

Lady Isobella nodded but did not smile, casting a look over her shoulder towards Lady Rosalyn before taking his offered arm.

"If you do not wish to, then I would be glad to return you to Lady Granville's company." Not wanting her to feel in any way obliged, Amos waited for her to look up at him, relieved when a smile crossed her face.

"I should be glad to walk with you," she said quietly. "I am only surprised that Lady Rosalyn had to step away, but mayhap she has seen another acquaintance."

Or mayhap she wishes for us to walk together, Amos

thought silently, his lips curving. "Tell me, Lady Isobella, what is it like to be a bluestocking?"

She stopped short, pulling him back as he looked down at her, wondering at her surprise. When she said nothing, a flush touched his cheeks.

"Did I say something to upset you?"

"No, not at all." Blinking quickly, she shook her head as if to clear her thoughts. "No one has ever asked me such a direct question before."

He swallowed. "I hope I am not too forward in my questions."

Her smile returned. "Not in the least. If you are genuinely interested, then I would be glad to share with you."

With relief pouring into him and a gentle pleasure in his heart when she took his arm again, Amos nodded. "Please. I should very much like to know."

"It is difficult." Her eyes lifted to his, but then returned to the path as they walked slowly along it. "I have such a love of reading and of learning, my desire to further what I know near insatiable at times... but to know that society, on the whole, despises ladies such as myself makes it very trying indeed."

"I can imagine there must be a trial in that," he murmured, looking at her. "Society has many difficult opinions, does it not?"

Her lips lifted, but there was a sadness there. "Indeed." She took a breath and then smiled. "I have been blessed with good friends, however. Friends who are very much like me."

"Oh?"

She looked up at him, her eyes shining. "We have

managed to use our intelligence to solve a few mysteries this Season. That has been a blessing."

A little surprised, Amos returned her smile, thinking all the more highly of her. Using her intelligence and wit to help others was remarkable indeed. "And have you always been interested in reading and the like?"

Interest sparked in her eyes. "No, not always. I only began to read a few years ago, when... well, when I returned from the London Season. My mother resides in the house still, along with my brother and his wife. During the winter, I began to read and that, I suppose, built a love for learning within my heart. I read so very much, my mother would often berate me for having a book at the dining table!" Red infused her cheeks. "I should not want you to think me improper but – "

Amos laughed quietly, making her smile. "It is *very* improper, Lady Isobella, but I can well understand it. My own sister would sometimes take the novel she was reading to the dining room when she was breaking her fast. My father would be quite irritated whenever she did such a thing, but it did not stop her!"

The sound of her laughter mingling with his made Amos' heart twist. It was such a beautiful sound, and his interest in her grew in an instant. No longer could he hold himself back, nor did he *wish* to hold himself back from her. If there was an interest there – and there most certainly was – then why did he need to worry what society might think of him calling upon her to take tea?

"Lady Isobella," he began, stopping in his walk and turning to look at her. "I was wondering if you would permit me to call upon you one afternoon."

The smile on her face instantly disappeared, the light in her eyes fading to shadow. There was no immediate smile, no blush darkening her cheeks. Instead – and much to his confusion and doubt – she appeared upset at his remark, given the way she turned her gaze from his, her eyebrows lowering.

"Good afternoon, Your Grace! Lady Isobella, good afternoon to you also!"

Before she could answer him, before anything more could be said, a gentleman strode towards them across the grass, his eyes fixed on Lady Isobella.

"I see that you are both enjoying a walk," Lord Preston said although his gaze was fixed to the lady instead of turning to them both. "A fine day for it, I quite agree!"

Amos cleared his throat, wondering how he might tell Lord Preston that he was interrupting the conversation between himself and the lady, only for Lady Isobella to speak and interrupt him.

"It is, yes," she said, removing her hand from his arm entirely. "I was, however, about to return to my sister in law, for we will soon have to make our way back to the house in preparation for this evening."

"And what occasion is it that you are attending?" Lord Preston wanted to know, shifting his stance slightly so that he looked away from Amos and towards Lady Isobella instead. "Might I be fortunate enough to be attending the very same one, I wonder?"

When she smiled, Amos noticed there was no brightness in her expression, no warmth there any longer. His question about calling upon her appeared to have brought about more shadow than sunshine.

"It is the Marquess of Devon's ball," she said, as Lord Preston let out a loud exclamation. "I have heard it is always an exceptional evening."

"You have heard correctly!" Lord Preston said, enthusiasm in every word. "Then I shall make certain to find you there and sign my name to one of your dances, of course."

Her smile did not linger. "You are very kind, Lord Preston."

"I shall return you now to Lady Granville," Amos interjected, aware that he was bringing a sharp end to the conversation between them but, at the very same time, disliking just how forward Lord Preston had been to not only interrupt them but speak only to Lady Isobella thereafter! "Do excuse us, Lord Preston."

The lady smiled briefly and then, much to Amos' relief, took his arm again. They walked in silence, a tension there that had not been there before. Amos could not understand it, wondering what it was he had done that had shattered the growing connection between them both.

"Thank you, Your Grace." As they drew near to Lady Granville, Lady Isobella stopped and then took her hand from his arm. "I enjoyed walking with you today."

The question on his mind, the one he *wanted* to ask her, stayed firmly behind his lips.

"Am I to see you this evening?" she ventured, looking up at him and then away just as quickly. "Are you to attend the ball?"

"I am, yes." Taking a breath, he pressed his lips together and then smiled. "If I might be as bold as Lord Preston, would I also be able to sign your dance card?"

"But of course." The answer came quickly enough, but there was no expression of happiness on her face, no enthusiasm in her response. "Thank you, Your Grace. Good afternoon."

Amos watched her as she walked away, seeing Lady Granville smile at her and then look towards him. With a nod, he turned on his heel and made his way directly back towards his carriage, having no interest in lingering here any longer. For whatever reason, asking to call upon her had broken their connection apart, seeming to upset her instead of pleasing her. Scowling, Amos rubbed one hand over his face as he walked, ignoring every other gentleman and lady in the park. What had he done that would make the thought of him coming to call so very dreadful? And why, he considered, did he feel her rejection so very painfully?

Chapter Nine

Isobella looked across the ballroom, her mind filled with the question the Duke of Exeter had asked her earlier that day. The other bluestockings were all talking and laughing around her, but she did not join them, too distracted to even think about what they were saying. The Duke's question, his desire to call on her, had frightened her.

It was a strange reaction, she considered, her gaze lingering on nothing at all, drifting here and there as she thought. A gentleman seeking to call upon a lady was just what was expected, she knew, but when he had asked to do that very thing, she had been near frozen with fright.

"Isobella?"

She started violently as Lady Amelia put a hand on her arm. "Oh, forgive me." Closing her eyes, she smiled weakly. "I was lost in thought."

"About the Duke?" Lady Amelia gave her a knowing smile. "Lady Rosalyn told me that she had left you to walk with him."

"Yes, she did."

Lady Amelia studied her for a moment or two. "She meant well. She does not know about your previous struggles."

"I am not angry with her for that," Isobella assured her. "Not at all."

"Then what troubles you?"

Isobella considered for a moment. Should she be honest with her friend or keep back all that had happened? After all, she had spent years slowly pushing down every bit of pain that had come about after her two failed Seasons, so she was more inclined to do the same here too.

"I am your friend," Lady Amelia reminded her, softly as if she could see into Isobella's mind and understand what she was thinking. "If there is something that troubles you, I would be glad to listen."

Pressing her lips flat, Isobella nodded slowly, convincing herself to be honest.

"It will help, I am sure."

Letting out a slow breath, Isobella swallowed hard. "The Duke of Exeter asked to call on me."

Lady Amelia's gasp was immediate.

"I – I did not answer him," Isobella continued, before her friend could say anything more. "I could not."

"Because you did not expect it?"

Isobella closed her eyes against a sudden swell of tears. "I was afraid to."

"Oh, my dear Isobella." Lady Amelia took a step closer to her but did not embrace her, perhaps aware that the other bluestockings would see and wonder what the problem was. "You have closed your heart so completely, have you not?"

"I have." Hearing her voice crack, Isobella took a few seconds to compose herself, refusing to cry in front of Lady Amelia. "I cannot trust him. I cannot trust *any* gentleman."

"Then you refuse him," Lady Amelia said, practically. "If that is what you have decided, then that is what you must do."

Isobella's throat constricted. "My brother would be most upset if he heard of it. My mother, too. That is the reason they have brought me back to London. To make a good match."

"And the Duke would be a good match, yes," Lady Amelia said, softly. "You do not have to let yourself fall in love with him, Isobella. It could be a match of practicality only."

The thought was still a terrifying one.

"I promised him that I would dance this evening," Isobella told her, aware of just how furiously her heart began to beat at the thought of being in his arms. "I do not want to. Nor do I want to dance with Lord Preston, but I have promised him also!"

Lady Amelia frowned, opened her mouth and then closed it again before looking away.

"What were you going to say?" Isobella asked, clutching at her friend's hand. "Please, tell me."

"Only this." Lady Amelia squeezed Isobella's hand gently. "I understand that you are afraid of losing your heart to a gentleman who will only break it apart in some way, but at the same time, I should hate to think of you lonely. To your eyes, it might seem that walking the path of spinsterhood would save you from a great deal of pain, but could there not also be sorrow and struggle in spinsterhood?"

Isobella looked away. "I am aware that there might well be difficulty, but – "

"What happens when your brother and his wife bring children into the world? I am sure you will be a doting aunt, but might there not also be a little sadness lingering in your own heart?"

I do not want to think about this, Isobella told herself, trying to block out her friend's words. *I cannot.*

For years, she had thought only about what she would do should a gentleman ever come to call upon her again, never once letting herself consider what the lonely years of being a spinster might do to her heart and mind. Now, however, Lady Amelia appeared to be quite determined to throw it out towards her regardless, forcing her to think upon it all the same.

"If you were to have a marriage of practicality, then you would never need to offer your heart to him," Lady Amelia concluded. "That way, you are safe and protected, are you not? You will never need to fear the agony of a broken heart and shattered trust, for there will not be that affection nor connection between you."

"That is not something I had considered before," Isobella said softly, looking down at her hands as they clasped tightly together. "I am afraid to even think about anything other than what I had already determined for my life."

Lady Amelia smiled quietly. "I can understand that, but there is sure to be more for you than this," she responded. "Let yourself think upon it, Isobella. The Duke of Exeter has a good reputation, excellent standing, and a fortune that will keep you in comfort all the days of your life. Those are good things, are they not?"

She nodded. "Yes, I suppose it is." Taking a long breath in, she set back her shoulders and looked directly back at Lady Amelia. "I will accept him then, I think."

"You will?" Lady Amelia beamed in delight.

"I will. It is only to take tea, however, nothing like

courtship or the like," Isobella stated, relieved that she now felt a little more at ease. "It is only a first step."

"But it is a good first step."

Isobella managed to smile. "Thank you for listening to me, Amelia. I am inclined to keep all my emotions and thoughts entirely to myself, but I can see that it has not done me as much good as I might have thought."

Lady Amelia's smile faded. "It is always good to share heavy burdens, I think. I do not know what I would do without the other bluestockings!"

"Nor I," Isobella admitted, looking to her left and smiling at the way her friends all laughed together. "I shall miss you all very much when the time comes for us to part ways."

Lady Amelia nodded and pressed Isobella's hand. "But it is not today that we must part, so let us not think of it."

"Lady Isobella! Good evening."

Isobella turned her head, ready to speak to the Duke of Exeter, ready to say to him that she was sorry for the way she had not answered his question about coming to call, only to look into the jolly face of Lord Preston. A little surprised at how her heart dipped low, she dropped into a quick curtsy. "Good evening, Lord Preston."

"I have come to claim my dance," he said, as two other gentlemen approached, one being Lord Broughton. "I hope you have not forgotten?"

"I have not," she answered, giving him her dance card without delay.

Lady Amelia moved forward. "Broughton!" she said, taking his arm. "You have come to dance with me also, I hope?"

The gentleman chuckled and lifted her hand, kissing the back of it. "Of course, my love. The waltz shall be mine,

I think!" He smiled then at Isobella, gesturing to the gentleman beside him. "Lady Isobella, might I introduce the Earl of Ryeland? Lord Ryeland, this is Lady Isobella. Her brother is the Earl of Granville."

The gentleman's eyes warmed at once. "I am acquainted with Lord Granville. I have not had the pleasure of being introduced to his sister as yet, however, so the pleasure is all mine." Bowing low, he came a step or two closer. "If Lord Preston would be so kind, I should also like to sign your dance card, Lady Isobella?" With a warm smile, he looked to Lady Amelia. "And yours also, if I might?"

A little surprised that the gentleman would be so eager to sign her dance card after only a few words of introduction, Isobella was quick to nod. "But of course. I thank you."

"The pleasure is mine." Lord Ryeland glanced at her, holding her gaze for just a moment before looking away, a hint of a smile gracing his lips. This sent something scurrying through Isobella's core, his look not only astonishing her but making her blush – something she had not done in many a year! When he returned her dance card to her, Isobella smiled but said nothing, wondering why this gentleman appeared to be so interested in her when they had only just been introduced! It was not as though Lord Broughton would befriend a scoundrel or a rogue, so he must be a gentleman of good standing, which, at least, was some comfort.

"Wonderful!" Lord Preston directed his gaze back towards Isobella. "I look forward to our dance, Lady Isobella."

Isobella nodded but said nothing. She was still waiting for the Duke of Exeter to appear, wondering when he would come to make his appearance known. What dance would he take? Would he want to dance the waltz with her again? Swallowing hard, she pushed the thought aside. If the Duke did such a thing, then the *ton* would certainly take all the more notice of his supposed attention towards her – and what then?

"Lord Broughton has told me a good deal about you, Lady Isobella." Lord Ryeland's eyes flickered with interest. "You are very learned, I hear."

Immediately, Isobella understood why the gentleman had been so interested in dancing with her. He had, it seemed, been informed about her by Lord Broughton who, no doubt, was doing so with the very best of intentions – namely to push her towards a suitable gentleman. "I do enjoy reading, yes."

"Not only novels!" Lord Broughton replied with a grin. "What is it that interests you at present, Lady Isobella?"

Isobella smiled briefly, a nervousness tumbling through her. Lord Broughton meant well, but she did not want to be connected to any gentleman. Spinsterhood was to be her path, and even this very amiable Lord Ryeland would do nothing to change that. "I am studying a little more about the animal kingdom."

"And birds, of course!" Lord Preston interjected, a broad smile on his face. "That is *my* area of interest, I confess, and I have been very eager indeed to share my knowledge with Lady Isobella. It is not very often that a young lady shows such an interest in such things!"

"That is because it is generally discouraged," Lady Amelia said, before Isobella could respond. "It is very refreshing to discover gentlemen who are not in the least bit concerned about such interests, however, and instead, seek to encourage them."

Lord Ryeland smiled but directed his attention back towards Isobella. "I am certainly not at all opposed to it. I think having a young lady who loves to learn and to read and to study means that there can be many more interesting conversations."

"Indeed, I quite agree!" Lord Preston exclaimed, his voice a little louder than before, as if to suggest he did not want to be forgotten. "It appears to me that many a gentleman can be disinclined towards gossip and whispers and even balls and soirees without too much notice from the *ton,* but a young lady who turns from all of that and seeks, instead, to expand her knowledge is given quite the rebuff! Why should it be that *she* is ignored and slighted when a gentleman is not?"

Isobella smiled, nodded, but inwardly felt herself squirm. Both of these gentlemen appeared to be very pleasant indeed, but she did not know what to do with their attentions. This conversation certainly appeared to be directed towards her, towards encouraging her to think well of both fellows and Isobella, uncertain what she ought to say or do, found herself looking down at her clasped hands, her breathing a little quicker now.

"I – I should take my leave," she said suddenly, lifting her head and looking straight at Lady Amelia. "I must go in search of my brother; he will be wondering where I am. After all, we did say that we were only to do a turn about the room!"

Lady Amelia nodded, her brow a little furrowed. "Of course. I will accompany you." She smiled at her betrothed when he offered to join them, excused herself from Lord Preston and Lord Ryeland – with Isobella doing the same – and then took Isobella's arm.

"Broughton does not know anything about your hesitancy when it comes to gentlemen," she murmured, as Lord

Broughton also took his leave of the other two fellows. "Do not think poorly of him, I beg you."

"Of course I do not," Isobella answered quickly, speaking in a low voice. "I know very well that he was thinking very kindly of me."

"And Lord Ryeland does appear to be a good fellow."

Isobella glanced at her friend, then, seeing Lord Broughton hurrying to join them, only smiled. It did not matter if Lord Ryeland *was* an excellent fellow, she could not let herself trust anyone again.

"There we are, then." Lord Broughton took his betrothed's arm and then smiled at Isobella. "You have more than one dance this evening, yes?"

"And you are still waiting for the Duke of Exeter," Lady Amelia said, with a slight lift of her eyebrows. "You will be much in demand, I am sure."

Even if I do not wish to be. Isobella opened her mouth to say something, only for a loud cry to catch not only her attention but also the attention of many near to them. They stopped in their progress across the ballroom, each head turning in the direction of the French doors. A young lady rushed out of them, her hands flailing, tears pouring down her cheeks, with another young lady following thereafter. Isobella saw her catch the first young lady, throwing her arms around her while the first began to sob.

"Goodness gracious, whatever has happened?" Lady Amelia exclaimed, looking wide-eyed at the scene before them. "I do hope both of those young ladies are quite all right?"

"Indeed," Isobella murmured, watching them both still as other gentlemen and ladies began to come inside, walking through the French doors in groups of two or three. Some went to speak to the young ladies, others moved away quickly but glanced over their shoulders as they did so.

"There!"

One of the young ladies – the second one who had come in – pointed at the doorway as three gentlemen walked through it, one after the other. She immediately began to sob, the first joining her as she began to weep also.

"They cannot be pointing at the Duke of Exeter, can they?" Lord Broughton's voice was low, his brow furrowed, and catching her breath, Isobella realized that one of the three gentlemen who had walked through the door was, in fact, the Duke of Exeter. He was walking through the crowd now, seemingly nonchalant, but, at the same time, many guests were turning their heads to look at him.

"He would not have done something dreadful, would he?" Isobella asked, her heart beginning to clamor as Lady Amelia began to frown. "He is a *Duke*."

"And dukes can very often do as they please, if they so wish," her friend said, darkly. "Let us hope he is not responsible for whatever it is that has taken place."

Isobella watched the Duke walk away, her heart thudding wildly. Had she misjudged the Duke of Exeter? Thus far, he had seemed like an excellent gentleman, but, mayhap now, his character was a good deal less than it had seemed.

I should not care, she told herself, turning away from the scene and beginning to walk across the room again to find her brother. *I should not care one jot about the Duke of Exeter.*

Her eyes closed briefly as her heart twisted. Yes, she might tell herself repeatedly that she had no need to care about anything that the Duke of Exeter did or said but the truth was, she *did*... and that was a very concerning thing indeed.

Chapter Ten

I *wonder where Lady Isobella is?*

Amos made his way through the ballroom carefully, nodding and smiling at various acquaintances but quickly ignoring any young lady beckoning at him to come and join their conversation. He did not want to stop at any conversation, did not want to linger with anyone. The only person on his mind was Lady Isobella.

After their walk together in the park, he had come to the determined conclusion that he was going to seek to court her. His question, however, had been left unanswered, that strange awkwardness building between them – an awkwardness that he had struggled to comprehend. Thus, even though it was perhaps not the right course of action, Amos had decided he would seek her out and apologize for his forwardness, in the hope that she might not pull away from him. If the thought of him coming to call upon her was so troubling, then mayhap he should linger only in conversations here and there before moving any further forward. The last thing he desired was for her to move away from him.

It is strange just how quickly she has taken hold of me, he thought to himself, making his way to the French doors in the hope that she was out in the gardens. *Suddenly now, I can think of no one else other than her.*

"Oh, Your Grace! Good evening. How pleasant to see you again."

Amos was forced to stop, bowing low so that Lady Clara would not see the grimace crossing his face. "Good evening, Lady Clara."

She set her hand on his arm, coming a little closer to him – closer than she might have dared had they been inside the ballroom. The darkness here hid a good deal more than otherwise might have been accepted. "Let me introduce you to two of my *very* dear friends. Your Grace, might I present Lady Sara and Miss Abernathy."

Amos bowed again, wishing he had not been forced to stop and speak with Lady Clara. He most certainly did not need to have two more young ladies fawning over him, not when he had already one young lady in mind. "A pleasure, of course."

"Miss Abernathy is sister to the Viscount Hodgeson and Lady Sara's father is the Earl of Dumfries."

Putting on a smile, Amos nodded to both the young ladies. "How very good to meet you both."

"And to meet you," Lady Sara said, her voice a little soft, her eyes glinting in the moonlight. "Pray, tell us, are you to dance this evening? Miss Shelton has told us that, on occasion, you have chosen *not* to do so, greatly disappointing a good many young ladies!"

Are they both just as forward as she? Amos' smile faded. "I am not certain as yet," he said, in clipped tones, hoping this would dissuade them from asking him anything further. "I have only just arrived, and there are one or two acquaintances I very much wish to speak to this evening. That is my goal at present."

The ladies all glanced at each other, with Miss Abernathy the first to speak. "Might I ask who they are? Mayhap we would be able to assist you."

Having no desire to reveal that he was eager to speak to Lady Isobella, Amos forced a smile, beginning to move slowly away from them all. "Thank you for your offer of assistance, Miss Abernathy. I am sure I will find them soon enough! Do excuse me."

The disappointment wrote itself on their faces in an instant, leaving Amos with an even greater urge to rush from them. Miss Shelton had already reached out once to grasp at his arm, and he could have no assurance that she would not do so again! Moving to the other side of the gardens, Amos ran one hand over his face, letting out a slow breath as he set aside his frustration. Miss Shelton and her friends were persistent, determined, and more than a little forward! He had to pray that they would not come to spy him out again later that evening.

"Oh, Your Grace! You have come to join us, I see."

Amos blinked, his shoulders dropping. He had not seen Lady Deborah near him. "Lady Deborah, good evening."

"My mother is just there." She waved one hand carelessly to her left. "You recall Lady Victoria, yes?"

"Yes, of course." Amos bowed, sweat breaking out across his forehead, his chest tightening with the feeling of being trapped. "Good evening to you also."

Lady Victoria smiled but did not drop into a curtsy as Amos might have expected. "Your Grace, good evening."

Smiling quickly, Amos wondered silently how he might escape this conversation and return inside. It was clear now that Lady Isobella was not present outside, which meant he had no cause to linger.

"Are you to disappoint us again, I wonder?" Lady Victoria continued when Amos did not say anything. "You are not to dance, mayhap?"

"I am not certain as yet," Amos responded, wondering what made the thought of dancing with him so very appealing. "I may yet."

"You shall have to be quick to make your decision, Your Grace!" Lady Deborah laughed, tapping his arm lightly, her eyes sparkling. "What if you discover that there are to be no young ladies left to dance with you? What if all their dances are taken and you are left quite despondent?"

"Then despondent I shall be," Amos replied, with a forced smile. "I should excuse myself, for – "

A sudden sound caught his attention, ripping the rest of his words from his mouth. It sounded like a cry of some kind, albeit quieter than a scream. Had someone been surprised in some way?

"I presume someone did not stay close to the lamps," Lady Deborah remarked dismissively. "The paths through the garden are not well-lit. It is much more preferable to remain here, I am sure."

Amos pulled his lips to one side, looking over to the darker part of the gardens. "I hope there is no one in some sort of distress."

"I am sure there is not." Lady Deborah shifted her stance so that she stood a little more directly in front of him, blocking his view of the garden. "Now, Your Grace – "

"It did sound a little troubling to me." Lady Victoria frowned, her eyes going to Amos, searching his face. "It was as if someone had been startled."

"Because they did not stay close to the lamps."

Sounding exasperated now, Lady Deborah sighed heavily. "Come now, we need not worry, I am sure."

The sound came again, a second time, and Amos' skin prickled. "Mayhap I should go to make certain all is well. Even if someone has only been startled by something, it would be best, mayhap, to make certain all is well."

Lady Victoria nodded, her eyes flicking from his face to the dark garden and then back again. "It would certainly make me feel a good deal more at ease if you would. We do not want anyone to be in distress."

"Indeed not."

Lady Deborah let out a heavy, almost plaintive sigh. "I am quite sure you are both making a good deal of fuss over nothing at all. Whatever it is, there will be nothing whatsoever to worry about."

"You cannot be sure of that," Lady Victoria said, quickly. "If the Duke wishes to go, then I am quite supportive of that."

His mind made up, Amos began to walk away from Lady Deborah and Lady Victoria, still hearing Lady Deborah's complaints ringing towards him. The garden grounds were not particularly well lit aside from the one area he had been standing in, which gave him some concern. Whatever that cry had been, he had to agree with Lady Victoria – there was some concern there.

"Is everything quite all right?" he called, the moonlight the only way to light his path now. Stumbling over something, he let out an exclamation of frustration, only to stand tall again.

A shadow moved.

"I do not mean to interrupt," he said, a sudden flush of embarrassment overwhelming him. What if he was interrupting a moment between a gentleman and a lady who might, unbeknownst to him, be already engaged and stealing only a brief few minutes together? "I must know that all is well, however. I heard something and – ooft!"

Something smacked into him, hard, making him stumble back and knocking into what felt like a thousand needles stabbing him at once. Someone rushed past him, then another. Whispers floated by him as Amos struggled to regain his standing. Every time he put a hand back, something stung his skin, making it rather painful to stand.

"I am nothing but a fool," he muttered to himself, managing now to right himself and brushing his hands down his clothes. With a sigh, he took a breath, closed his eyes, and then let it out, giving himself a slight shake. He would have to return to Lady Deborah and Lady Victoria and assure them that all was well. Evidently, it had been just as he had feared, he *had* interrupted a moment between lovers. There was nothing here of note at all.

"Lady Victoria?" Coming back to where the ladies had been standing, Amos did not find them. Frowning, he made his way back to the ballroom, walking through the French doors as two other gentlemen followed him.

A frown tugged at his forehead as he stepped inside. A young lady was pointing in the direction of the French doors – Lady Clara, was it not? Walking away from her just as quickly as he could for fear that she, too would pull him into conversation, Amos tried to melt into the crowd but, for some strange reason, many a gentleman and lady were staring at him. Frowning, he continued on his way, wondering just where he might find Lady Isobella.

"Your Grace?"

He turned, seeing not one but three young ladies staring back at him, their faces a little white. "Yes?" uncertain if he was acquainted with any of them, he tried quickly to remember their names. "Lady... ?"

"Lady Margaret." The one who had spoken to him at the first, the one whose eyes were very large indeed now, staring up at him as she spoke, blinked rapidly. "What happened, might I ask?"

"Happened?" Amos, unsure as to what he was being asked, looked back at Lady Margaret in confusion. "I do not understand."

"With Lady Clara and Lady Sara," she said, turning a little so as to gesture behind her. "They both rushed in and said that you – well, that there was some commotion outside."

A heavy weight dropped into Amos' stomach. Was this why everyone was looking at him? Did they believe that he had something to do with whatever had occurred? "I am afraid I cannot tell you, Lady Margaret," he said, as she and her friends all glanced at each other. "I was not present with them, you see. I was, instead, looking in the gardens for... "

"For what?" The lady lifted an eyebrow, and a cold hand gripped Amos' heart. What could he say? If he stated that he had been searching for the sound of someone in distress, would they not then think that he was responsible for the commotion – even more so than they clearly already did?

"For the stars," he lied, with what he hoped was a confident smile. "The gardens were very well lit, so I took myself to a quieter part in the hope of seeing some of the stars. They are very bright this evening!"

This did not appear to convince Lady Margaret for she sniffed once, then lifted her chin. "Is that so, Your Grace?"

"It is. I am sorry for whatever has happened to Lady Clara, but I can assure you it has nothing to do with me."

Thinking it best to bring the conversation to an end, he bowed to them all and kept a smile on his face. A smile he most certainly did not feel. "Do excuse me. I must go in search of my friend."

Stepping away, he kept his head low as he began to stride towards the door, worrying now that something amiss had occurred and that he was, for some reason, to be given the blame for it all. To leave the ball might make him appear guilty, yes, but until he knew precisely what it was he was being blamed for, Amos did not know what else to do.

"Did you find her?" Lord Galbraith stepped in front of him, a broad grin on his face. "Your expression is a little dismal, so I must fear you have not."

Amos looked back at his friend. "Galbraith, something has happened."

The smile slid from Lord Galbraith's face at once. "What do you mean?"

Looking over his shoulder, Amos scowled. "I cannot say but there seems to have been some upset out in the gardens." He looked back at Lord Galbraith. "I was present and I had a very forward young lady come to speak with me, suggesting that I was in some way responsible!"

"That is preposterous!"

"I appreciate your trust in me." Amos' heart began to quicken. "But I am not certain what I should do. Remain here and wait to see what is said of me, or return home."

Lord Galbraith pressed his lips into a thin line, then stepped to one side. "I suggest you go to Whites or some such thing. Do *not* return home, but let yourself be seen there. To make your way home would suggest you have done something wrong, but to go to Whites means you can tell others present that you enjoyed the ball and then thought to find a little quietness in Whites thereafter. That way, the *ton* will think that you have made your way to Whites simply because you have had quite enough of the ball!"

Amos nodded. "Very well."

"I will find out what I can and then come to join you," Lord Galbraith told him, firmly. "Wait there for me, no matter how late it gets."

"I shall." With a word of thanks, Amos made his way from the ballroom without a word to anyone. He kept his head high and smiled at this person and then the other, making sure not to rush his steps. All the while, however, his heart was pounding, his fear growing as he battled worry and doubt. What was it that had happened to Lady Clara? And why did so many seem to think *him* responsible?

Chapter Eleven

L ord Ryeland smiled up at Isobella as she served his cup of tea. "I thank you."

"But of course." She sat down again quickly, trying to ignore the look of delight that had set itself upon Louisa's face at the arrival of Lord Ryeland, a look which had not yet dissipated in any way.

"I wonder what you have been reading today?" Lord Ryeland asked, his smile lingering as he continued to hold her gaze, unsettling Isobella a little. "I know from Lord Broughton that you are always with a book in your hand! Just as Lady Amelia is also, I understand."

Isobella could not help but smile at this. "Indeed. Given that we are both bluestockings, it should not be in the least bit surprising to anyone that we have books with us almost all of the time!"

Lord Ryeland chuckled. "Have you found your reading of great interest to you of late?"

"I have." Warming to the subject, Isobella told him of the recent discoveries of some new and exotic animals she had read about, seeing his eyebrows lift in surprise. "Some of them do sound quite fantastic," she admitted, as he reached for his teacup. "I was very glad to know of them."

"Remarkable indeed!" he exclaimed, as Louisa sat there, doing nothing other than smiling at them both. "I am sure that Lord Preston will be able to pique your interest all the more with his knowledge of birds." His smile became a little crooked. "He did not stop talking about them all last evening, once the ball was over and we found ourselves in Whites."

Wondering if this was meant as a slight against Lord Preston, Isobella said nothing and sipped at her tea instead.

"I admit that I was very surprised indeed to see the Duke of Exeter at Whites last evening," Lord Ryeland continued, clearly unwilling for there to be even a breath of silence. "After all that took place, I was astonished that he would think to set himself out in front of society!"

"All that took place?" Louisa asked before Isobella could do so. "What do you mean by that?"

Isobella glanced at her sister in law, then looked back to Lord Ryeland, who was now frowning, watching his cup of tea as if there was something quite interesting within it. "There was an upset with Lady Clara," she said, having learned the lady's name the previous evening. "Her friend, Lady Sara, was also involved. I do not know the particulars, but I believe they were both very upset indeed."

Lord Ryeland snorted gently, making Isobella shoot her gaze back towards him in surprise. "They had every right to be! I can understand that a Duke of the realm believes himself to be of a higher standing than everyone else and can do just as he pleases, but to attempt to... *coerce* a young lady to join him in the dark of the gardens is disgraceful behavior for any gentleman, including a Duke!"

A kick to Isobella's stomach made her breath hitch.

Could it be that the Duke of Exeter had done such a thing? She had thought she knew his character somewhat, and never once had he given the impression of being arrogant, selfish, and willing to do just as he pleased!

"Goodness, that is dreadful news indeed," Louisa murmured, as Isobella looked down at her tea again. "Are they quite sure it was the Duke responsible for such a thing?"

Lord Ryeland shrugged. "It was the word of both Lady Clara *and* Lady Sara, so it must be true."

"Although it was very dark in the gardens," Isobella found herself saying, garnering looks of surprise from both Lord Ryeland and her sister in law. "There are occasions when gentlemen have been mistaken for another fellow entirely, and I do want to make certain I am being very careful in what I believe to be the truth."

Lord Ryeland eyed her carefully, then nodded. "That, I think, is very wise, Lady Isobella. It is always best to be entirely sure about such things, especially when someone's reputation is involved!"

"Precisely," Isobella said, a little more loudly than she had meant. "I am sorry to hear that Lady Clara and Lady Sara were upset, however. That must have been very difficult for them."

"From what I heard, they both had to return home from the ball nearly at once," Lord Ryeland said, with a grimace. "A great pity to hear that their evening was ruined in such a way."

Louisa glanced at Isobella and then nodded. "We can only hope that it will not keep them back from society for too long."

"Indeed." Lord Ryeland rose to his feet, the allotted time for calling now coming to an end. "Thank you for the tea and the excellent conversation, Lady Isobella, Lady Granville. I must take my leave of you now, though I hope to see you again very soon." This last part of his remark was directed solely at Isobella, and before she could think of what she *ought* to say, what was on her heart came directly out towards him.

"Thank you for calling, Lord Ryeland. I do not think our acquaintance will continue on any further, however."

He blinked, his smile crumpling. "I beg your pardon?"

Isobella blinked, heat burning up through her as she tried to understand not only what she had said but why she had said it. "Thank you for calling," she said again, a little numbly. "Good afternoon."

Lord Ryeland frowned, opened his mouth to say something, and then seemed to think better of it. Once he had gone, Isobella sank down slowly onto her chair, her thoughts fixed solely upon the Duke of Exeter and what it was he had supposedly done. Her heart was a little heavy with that thought, and as she sank back down into her seat, she could not prevent a small sigh from escaping her.

"That was a little... forward."

She glanced at Louisa, wondering if there was a hint of chagrin in her voice. "Yes, it was. I do not know why I spoke so, but I am not inclined towards his company."

"No?"

Isobella shook her head, and they lapsed into silence for a short while. After a short time, her sister in law leaned towards her. "I am sorry," she said quietly. "The Duke of Exeter did appear to be interested in your company, and I can imagine that this news must have been something of a shock. Mayhap that is why you pushed Lord Ryeland away."

"I have no intention of stepping back from the Duke

just because of a rumor," Isobella said quickly, only for heat to rise up her chest and into her neck at Louisa's lifted eyebrows. "What I mean to say is that my friendship with him will not be set aside simply because I have heard something untoward about him. I would do the same with any connection, any acquaintance."

This made Louisa smile. "Yes, I think that you would. I perhaps should not have jumped to the belief that he is as guilty as Lord Ryeland suggested."

Isobella bit her lip, looking away. The worry that the Duke *had* done something was sitting on her mind, weighing her down. She did not want to think him guilty after only the word of Lord Ryeland but nor did she want to think that she knew everything about the Duke's character and understood all that he was. She might very well have made a mistake in thinking so well of him, but nor could she step back from him without being entirely certain of his guilt.

"You are going to be late if you do not leave soon." Louisa touched Isobella's arm, pulling her out of her concerning thoughts. "You are to call upon Lady Rosalyn, are you not?"

"Yes, yes, of course." Getting to her feet quickly, Isobella drew in a deep breath and then smiled. Lord Ryeland's visit had been unexpected, but she still had enough time to go and meet with the other bluestockings. "Thank you, Louisa."

"I do hope Lord Ryeland calls again," her sister in law said, with a glint in her eye. A glint that spoke of hope and of planning a wedding that Isobella did not herself want. "He does seem very pleasant and is *quite* contented with you being a bluestocking."

"Mmm." Saying nothing more, Isobella made her way

from the room, but as she stepped into the hallway, her shoulders dropped and her eyes closed for only a moment. She did not *want* Lord Ryeland to call again, did not want anyone to show any sort of interest in her. She was to be a spinster; she had decided that her future was to be one of being alone.

And yet... the Duke is in my thoughts.

Isobella swallowed hard, pushing that aside and making her way to her bedchamber so she might prepare herself for going to call on Lady Rosalyn. The matter with the Duke of Exeter would come to light soon enough, and she would not need to do anything to search out the truth. Not even if she wished to.

"I did hear that." Miss Trentworth pulled her lips to one side for a few moments, then shook her head. "I am not inclined to listen to gossip, but there is certainly the chance of it being true. A Duke is, by their title, often considered to be free from society's scrutiny in many ways, simply because of how high his standing is."

Isobella frowned. "I did not think that the Duke of Exeter was like that," she said, softly. "He did not give the impression that he was in any way arrogant or inclined towards doing such a terrible thing." She looked down at her hands in her lap. "That does not mean that I think myself correct in my belief about him, however. I understand I could be wrong."

The other bluestockings said nothing, and Isobella's heart twisted. She wished she could speak alone with Lady Amelia, knowing that her friend would understand the confusion in her heart and mind and realizing that, in doing so, she would unburden herself a little.

"I have heard something more, though it is again only a rumor." Miss Sherwood winced as Isobella looked at her sharply. "An acquaintance of mine informed me this morning that there are those who say that the Duke of Exeter has no fortune whatsoever! That he lives in poverty but pretends only to have wealth." She wrinkled her nose. "I do not know where such stories come from, and I certainly do not think that it is true. It is only something that I have heard."

Isobella looked at each bluestocking in turn but saw no belief of this shining in their eyes. They knew well enough the difficulties that society could place upon them all, understood the pain that came with whispers and rumors being believed.

"It is a strange tale to tell about the Duke of Exeter," Miss Trentworth mused. "Why should someone say that he has no fortune?"

"I could not say," Isobella replied, aware that she was the one who best knew the Duke of Exeter. "He does not flaunt his wealth but nor does he give the impression that he has any difficulty financially. It is not as though he is seeking out young ladies with vast dowries!" *Because most certainly, whilst my dowry is more than satisfactory, it is not enormous by any means.* She bit her lip. *He did wish to call on me. That must say something, at least... unless I have misjudged that also.*

Silence filled the room for a few moments, only for a knock to break it. Lady Rosalyn called for the servant to enter.

"Lady Isobella, there is a note for you." The footman came towards Isobella directly and handed her the note, making Isobella's stomach twist with worry. Had something happened with her brother? Was it Louisa? Opening the note, she read the few short lines quickly... and her mouth dropped open in astonishment.

Silence came from the other bluestockings as Isobella read the few lines again, a quiet exclamation coming from her as she took in what was being asked.

"We are all terribly eager to hear what it is that you have there, Isobella." Lady Amelia was the first to speak, a dash of color in her face. "I hope nothing is wrong?"

Isobella shook her head, folding up the note. "It is from the Duke of Exeter," she said, as her friends responded with astonishment. "He came to see if I was at the house, but was informed that I had come here. Such was his desire to speak with me that he sent a note."

"To speak with you?" Lady Amelia's eyes rounded. "Goodness, he is very eager indeed, is he not?"

Isobella looked down at the folded note. "It is not only I that he seeks to speak with," she said, taking in a deep breath and then releasing it again, setting her shoulders back as she looked around at her friends. "He begs to talk with me about what happened last evening at the ball, about what is being said of him. Thereafter, he says, he hopes that we will all help him work out this mystery so that he might restore his reputation."

"Then he states he is innocent," Miss Sherwood murmured as hope filled Isobella's heart, making her aware of just how much these rumors about him had affected her. "He must believe that there is more to this than we can understand."

Isobella nodded. "Indeed."

"Then you will speak to him?"

There was not even the smallest hesitation. "Yes, of course I shall."

Lady Amelia's eyes caught hers, and Isobella, feeling a

flush of warmth begin to rise up all over again, only lifted her shoulders and let them fall. She could not explain to her friend all that she felt at the present moment, not when the others did not know of her confusion, doubt, and now, relief... and especially when she did not fully understand it herself! An urgency flooded her, but she stayed where she was, unwilling to show her friends just how much the Duke's note had impacted her. To rise now and to hurry off to see him would bring many a lifted eyebrow, and Isobella did not want that.

"Is he not waiting for you?" Lady Amelia's question made the heat in Isobella's chest grow. "If you wish, I can join you? I have my maid and you have yours, so there would be nothing improper about it."

"Though you could not be seen entering the Duke's townhouse," Lady Rosalyn said, quickly. "That will bring yet more rumors, I am sure."

Isobella hesitated, aware of the desire within her to have this conversation as quickly as she could, while at the same time, heeding the warning from Lady Rosalyn. "I think I shall write to him and suggest a meeting," she said, slowly, thinking through what she might say. "It would have to be at a place and a time when the *ton* would not be about, when they would not see."

"Meaning they could not whisper," Miss Sherwood added, as Isobella nodded. "Then why do you not suggest a carriage ride? Perhaps in the early morning?"

"Or in the afternoon? Lord Waverley and I could take a carriage ride, and you could both join us? I could have Lord Waverley stop for him first, and you could meet us in your own carriage somewhere a little less populated." Miss Trentworth bit her lip. "It would take some planning, but it could be done."

This sounded a little clandestine, but given the situation and the care Isobella knew she would have to take, it was a wise suggestion. "Yes, it would be the best course of action."

Miss Trentworth nodded. "Then why do you not write to the Duke now? That way, the plan will have been made and you will both be a little more at ease."

Wondering if her concern and curiosity was written into her expression, Isobella rose and made her way to the writing desk, choosing to do precisely as Miss Trentworth had suggested. It would ease her mind although she was fully aware that her curiosity would linger.

It will not be too long until we can speak, she wrote, finishing her letter. *I do hope that this suggestion is agreeable to you. If there is truth to be found, Your Grace, then the bluestocking book club will find it. I can assure you of that.*

Chapter Twelve

Earlier that same afternoon

Amos paced up and down the drawing room, pushing one hand and then the other through his hair. "You are telling me that Lady Clara blames *me* for the attack upon her person?"

Lord Galbraith nodded, watching him from where he sat, one hand playing about his mouth as if he did not want to say what he had to. "I am afraid so."

"But how can that be?" Amos asked, stopping sharply and turning to look at his brother-in-law. "I did nothing wrong! I spoke with the lady, but did not *once* go near her. Nor did I advance upon her! Why should she say such a thing?"

With a sigh, Lord Galbraith lifted his shoulders. "Mistaken identity, mayhap? That is the only thing I can think."

"It seems very strange to me that she would think to blame me when I was not anywhere near her," Amos

113

protested, beginning to pace again. "This is truly dreadful! Whatever am I to do?"

When he turned to look at Lord Galbraith, the hesitancy on the man's face gave him pause. With a heaviness in his soul, Amos paused in his pacing for the second time and turned to face him. "What else is there?"

"I have heard a rumor or two," Lord Galbraith told him, his words stumbling over each other just a little. "I do not know why this is being said or where it comes from, but stories are being spread through the *ton*. I say stories because they are entirely fictional!"

"What is being said?"

Lord Galbraith let out a hiss through his teeth, then looked away. "I heard these two things only last evening," he said, not turning his gaze back towards Amos. "The first is that you are seeking a bride, but that she must have a vast dowry."

"Dowry?" Amos repeated, a little confused. "Why should I need such a thing?"

"Because you are supposedly quite without funds," Lord Galbraith told him, his eyebrows sitting low over his eyes, shadows dancing in his gaze. "You are impoverished, or so the *ton* have been told."

Amos closed his eyes, then pinched the bridge of his nose.

"You are, evidently, a gambler without restraint. You have lost a great deal of your wealth to the card table *and* have spent your coin in establishments that are a little less than reputable."

Horror struck, Amos sat down heavily, his whole being feeling heavy with the shock of what he had been told.

"This was only whispered about last evening, from what I can tell," Lord Galbraith finished, sounding apologetic as though he regretted having to be truthful on such a weighty matter as this. "I do not know where such a story has come from, and I certainly have not heard it before. I am sorry to have to tell you such a thing, my friend."

Closing his eyes, Amos dropped his head forward, his chin on his chest. "Goodness. I do not know what to do."

The silence that came from Lord Galbraith told Amos that his brother-in-law did not know what to advise either. Steadying his breathing, Amos kept his eyes shut as he clasped his hands in front of him, trying to ascertain what he ought to do next.

"I am sorry," Lord Galbraith said again as if somehow this was his doing. "I know that none of what has been said of you is true, but the *ton* will cling to it, I am afraid."

"I – I will be ruined."

Lord Galbraith shut his eyes. "Your reputation may be stained, yes."

"More than that!" Panic gripped him. "This stain will spread through London, it will touch everyone that is connected with me!" Shoving both hands through his hair, he squeezed his eyes closed until they were almost painful. "My sister... my mother – even you, Galbraith."

His brother-in-law sighed. "The *ton* are relentless."

"I must fight this." Opening his eyes, he looked straight back at Lord Galbraith, his breathing uneven. "I cannot have them think such dreadful things of me!"

Lord Galbraith spread out his hands. "What can you do? You could speak to Lady Clara, but I doubt she will have much to say to you." His eyebrows lifted. "There may even be whispers of matrimony if you are not careful."

Fear tore through Amos. "I cannot marry her."

"I am not saying you will have to, but you *must* be cautious, my friend."

Swallowing at the ache in his throat, Amos tried to think clearly. In a single instant, his life had been darkened by shadows, threats pulling in towards him. He had done nothing wrong and yet, for some unbeknownst reason, false-hoods were being whispered about him.

And what will Lady Isobella think of me?

Her face swam in front of his closed eyes, and he caught his breath, a sudden realization of what his connection to Lady Isobella might now look like, once she heard of the rumors. Would she believe them? Would she turn away from him? As yet, he had not managed to discuss with her his desire to come to take tea but mayhap that was all nothing but smoke now!

His head lifted. "I must speak with her."

"With whom?" Lord Galbraith frowned. "Lady Clara?"

"No, no." Amos rose to his feet, beginning to pace again as he thought. "I must speak to Lady Isobella."

Lord Galbraith's shoulders slumped. "You fear that she will reject you because of this."

"Yes, but she is also a bluestocking," Amos said, turning to face him. "She told me that she and her friends have worked to find out the truth in some other difficult situations. Why should I not ask her to assist me in this?"

Lord Galbraith ran one hand over his chin. "You are going to ask bluestockings to help you?"

"Why should I not? I can do nothing myself, and if there *is* someone spreading rumors about me, then I must learn who it is!" With a nod to his brother-in-law, Amos hurried towards the door. "And I must go now."

It was not until the following day that Amos had his desperate wish. The response from Lady Isobella had been encouraging, but being forced to wait until the following afternoon had been difficult. He had not slept well and had fought through frustration and upset before finally managing to sleep for an hour or two. Now, however, as he waited for Lord Waverley's carriage, Amos felt himself more awake than ever. His mind had not stopped spinning, his thoughts rushing from one side of his mind to the other ever since Lord Galbraith had told him what society believed of him.

"Lord Waverley, Miss Trentworth." Climbing into the carriage, Amos sat down beside Lord Waverley, relief pouring into him at their gentle expressions. "I cannot find enough words to thank you for all you are doing for me."

"But of course, Your Grace." Miss Trentworth offered him a warm smile as the carriage pulled away. "You must be very distressed, I am sure."

Even this remark gave Amos hope. "You believe me, then?"

"Of course." Lord Waverley was the one to speak, looking at Amos with a steady gaze. "We are all very aware of the power the *ton* has. The only question, I suppose, is why someone has turned on you in such a way."

Amos nodded, a knot in his throat. "Quite."

"Lady Isobella was very eager to speak with you," Miss Trentworth continued, as the carriage rumbled on. "She was glad to receive your note, I think."

Yet more relief swamped Amos, taking away a good deal of anxiety from his heart. He had been concerned that, despite his note to her and her response to him, there would still be some sort of distrust between them. "I wanted to write to her because I knew she – and yourself also, Miss Trentworth – had solved some difficulties for others."

Miss Trentworth nodded. "Yes, we have."

"The bluestocking book club," Lord Waverley replied, with a chuckle. "That was how I first met Miss Trentworth."

"Oh?"

There was no time for them to explain further, for the carriage began to pull to a stop. Amos' heart practically launched itself out of his chest as the door opened and, after only a moment, Lady Isobella climbed inside. She glanced at him as she sat down, a somewhat uncertain smile brushing her lips.

"Good afternoon to you all." Clearing her throat, she settled her hands on her lap as the carriage continued. "Lady Amelia is waiting in the carriage for me, but I cannot be long."

Lord Waverley chuckled, lightening the tension that Amos felt sparking between himself and Lady Isobella. "This is all very covert, is it not? I feel as though I ought to be taking some sort of secret to the Crown!"

"It is a little, yes," Lady Isobella said, with a wry smile. "But it must be this way."

"I am sorry for that," Amos began, only for Lady Isobella to shake her head.

"No, there is nothing for you to apologize for, Your Grace. Now, please." She sat a little further forward, her hands still clasped in front of her. "Tell us all."

Amos swallowed thickly, trying not to become distracted by the beauty of the lady. "Last evening, I was at the ball. I was looking for you, in fact, but went out into the gardens to see if were there." He continued, telling them about the conversations that had stopped him, then the sound that had concerned him.

"And you say that when you went back to find Lady Deborah and Lady Victoria, they were not there?" Lady

Isobell asked, as Amos nodded. "They were gone inside, then?"

"Which did seem a little strange to me, given that they were so very concerned about the noise we had heard – well, Lady Victoria was. Lady Deborah dismissed it."

Miss Trentworth frowned. "Strangely, they all hurried inside, but mayhap they were distracted by Lady Clara and the commotion there."

"If we spoke to them, would they be able to confirm that you were nowhere near Lady Clara?" Hope filled Lady Isobella's face, but Amos shook his head, dimming it instantly.

"They would be able to say where I was gone, but would not be able to confirm I had not gone back towards Lady Clara." He grimaced. "Unfortunately, the darkness conceals a good many things."

Lord Waverley snorted. "Indeed it does. In this case, it appears to have hidden the true perpetrator, for someone pursued Lady Clara and upset her, and then, for whatever reason, made her believe they were you!"

Releasing a slow breath, Amos looked from one face to the next. "Is that what you all think?"

Lady Isobella tilted her head just a fraction. "Are you trying to ask if we believe you, Your Grace?"

He nodded, his chest tightening.

"We do," she said quickly, reassurance in her smile. "I knew when I heard it that it could not be the truth. What I knew of your character spoke against that."

"And I am not impoverished either," Amos found himself saying, wanting her to believe that he was solvent and did not require a large dowry. "There have been other whispers about me also, it seems, but none of them are true either!"

Lady Isobella nodded but pulled her lips to one side, looking away from him and instead, out of the window, which had the curtain pulled, save for only one small sliver of light. Amos' heart began to thud wildly, hoping that one of them would have some notion as to what he ought to do next. He did not want his reputation to be ruined, and he certainly did not want the *ton* to think that he was a cruel, arrogant gentleman who did as he pleased. That sort of stain could ruin his name for generations.

"We must find out the truth." Lady Isobella took another moment, then turned to look Amos straight in the eye as the carriage continued on. "If everything you have told us is true, Your Grace, then the bluestockings will, I know, do all they can to reveal the truth not only to yourself but to society."

A tightness came into Amos' throat. "It *is* the truth," he said, trying to speak firmly but finding his heart aching with the confusion and the struggle that had come with these accusations. "I do not want the *ton* to believe me capable of such a thing! They will reject me, and even if I marry, even if I have an heir to this Dukedom, will not my son hear these whispers about me still? Will not my mother and sister be forced to endure it all?"

Lady Isobella did not look away from him. Her eyes held to his, a calmness there which centered him, helped him to breathe a little more easily. The more he looked into her eyes, the easier it became to quieten the whirling thoughts in his mind, the fears about what should happen in the future.

"We will find out why Lady Clara said such a thing," Lady Isobella told him firmly. "We will discover who has been whispering about your impoverished state, about your need for money. We have done such things before, and I am certain we shall do so again."

"You can have every confidence in the bluestockings," Lord Waverley told him, slapping Amos on the back. "They are quite remarkable."

"I believe it," Amos answered, his voice a little hoarse. "Thank you, Lady Isobella. Thank you, Miss Trentworth – and please, pass my thanks on to the others. I am grateful, truly. More than you can know."

Chapter Thirteen

"**Y**ou were very quick to trust the Duke."

Isobella glanced at Miss Trentworth as they walked through the park, Lady Amelia on her other side. "I could tell from the fear in his eyes and the dread in his voice that he spoke the truth."

"As could I," Miss Trentworth agreed, speaking softly perhaps for fear that someone in the park might hear them. "You are glad of it, I think."

Isobella looked back at the path rather than at her friend. "I am relieved that my judgment of his character was not in error."

Lady Amelia slipped her hand through Isobella's. "I am only glad that the meeting went well and that no one was seen," she said, drawing Miss Trentworth's attention away from Isobella and her response to the Duke. "Now, we are to go in search of Lady Clara, yes?"

Miss Trentworth nodded. "And I shall try to find Lady Sara. If we speak to them separately and then share what has been said, we might find a clue as to what truly took place. One of them might make a mistake in their recounting of what happened."

"A good thought." Isobella turned her head to look at Lady Amelia as they continued on their way, separating from Miss Trentworth. "I have not yet spoken to you about the Duke and his request as yet."

Lady Amelia smiled. "I can imagine that you are feeling a good many things at present."

Coming to a stop, all thought of Lady Clara flying from her mind, Isobella looked straight into Lady Amelia's eyes, choosing to be entirely honest. "When I heard the rumors about him, I must confess that my heart fell into dismay."

"And you were very ready to believe that he was not guilty in the least," Lady Amelia said, "although I do not say that to criticize you. I say it because I believe that you know the Duke's character fairly well and were, therefore, able to trust what you knew of him."

"I suppose that is true. I felt such great relief upon hearing his explanation of what happened." Her lips tugged to one side as she looked down at the ground at her feet, battling to find the right words to express herself. "What is happening to me, Amelia?"

Her friend's lips quirked. "I think you are already fully aware of it."

"But I *cannot*!" Isobella exclaimed, angry with herself for having such a weakness still. "Before all of this, I was quite determined to set myself back from the Duke. Then, in a single moment, when I hear that he is supposedly a scoundrel, I find myself all of a whirl about him! I should not have such confusion! I should not be battling doubt only to be overwhelmed with relief!" Breathing hard, she clenched her hands into fists, her emotions tumbling out of her now that she finally had the opportunity to release them. "I swore I should never let myself feel anything again, and now... " Squeezing her eyes closed, she let out a slow hiss of breath. "Now, I am nothing but a fool."

"No, you are not!" Lady Amelia grasped her hand, and Isobella opened her eyes, seeing her friend's earnest face. "Not in the least bit."

Isobella shook her head, her throat working to keep the tears back. "I am, Amelia. I have always told myself that I would never do so again, that I would never allow my heart to trust another time. I have been disappointed time and again, and I cannot let myself trust, not again. I just do not have enough heart left."

Something glistened in Lady Amelia's eyes and, without warning, she reached to embrace Isobella. Tears fought to free themselves from her lashes, but Isobella held them back, having no desire to be seen by so many of the *ton*.

"You have more than enough heart left," Lady Amelia said into Isobella's ear before stepping back, looking into Isobella's face. "I can well understand why you might wish to hide away, why you might want to remove yourself from this situation, but I must warn you, my friend, you will find yourself all the more sorrowful if you should do so."

Isobella shook her head. "No, I will have relief."

"I doubt that," Lady Amelia replied, a little more firmly now. "If you stay back from the Duke, if you refuse to acknowledge all that you feel, then there will not be any relief for you. Instead, there will be this constant agony and strife over all that you feel and all you wish to hide away. Then, mayhap some months or even years from now, you will find yourself with regret and sorrow over all that you stepped away from. You might think of these moments with a weighty sadness, one that you do not feel at present."

Frowning, Isobella looked away, aware that Lady Amelia's words were striking at her but having no desire to permit them to linger. "You think I will regret my decision?"

"When you think about what you might have had, if you had only let yourself begin to trust?" Lady Amelia nodded slowly. "Yes, I think you will. You have the hope of something wonderful here, Isobella. The Duke of Exeter clearly wants you to believe him, to trust that all that has been said of him is *not* true."

"That is only so that he might restore his reputation."

"Is it?" Lady Amelia smiled gently. "What if it is more than that? What if he wants his reputation restored *and* wants you to think well of him? What if his desire to have you work in this situation is because of how he feels?"

This did nothing to comfort Isobella but instead sent a great and terrible fear through her. She did not dare think of what the Duke might feel. Gentlemen had told her of their feelings before, and it had come to naught but heartbreak.

"You are not a fool, regardless of what you decide to do," Lady Amelia finished, releasing Isobella's hand. "Believe me in that, my dear friend. None of your pain and sorrow from the past is your responsibility. Your feelings at present are not foolish either, however! It is quite natural to be drawn to a gentleman and," she finished, with a warm smile, "the Duke of Exeter could be very different from the other gentlemen who injured you in such a way. He could be precisely what you have always hoped for."

That was a hope that ignited Isobella's heart, even though she did not wish it to do so. She wanted nothing more than to set the matter aside, to look at the Duke's difficulties with a calm, unemotional heart, but it seemed to be impossible for her.

"Come." Lady Amelia took Isobella's arm again. "Let us go and speak with Lady Clara and see what she has to say. To think about your own heart at present will, I fear, only bring you a good deal more confusion and upset. This might be a way to take your mind from your own circumstances."

Accepting her friend's suggestion, Isobella began to walk again, making their way toward the large gathering of both gentlemen and ladies. Hyde Park was very busy indeed, with more carriages arriving nearly every minute. There would soon be very little space for them to continue driving around the grounds, meaning that some would come to a complete stop so that their occupants might step out to speak with their acquaintances.

"I am not certain we will be able to find her here," Lady Amelia muttered, scowling. "There are so many others present, I fear we will struggle to spy her!"

"I think we will succeed." Isobella offered her friend a small, wry smile. "We need only go to where there are a large group of ladies, for they will all be eager to hear what she has to say, no doubt."

Lady Amelia's scowl faded. "You are quite right. The gossip mongers will be rife with eagerness to hear more of what she has to say about the Duke. I am sure, then, that we will find her."

Much to Isobella's relief, it did not take more than a few minutes for them to spy Lady Clara. She was standing with a large group of ladies and a few gentlemen, all of whom were listening to her with rapt attention. Isobella and Lady Amelia sidled in amongst them, with Isobella seeking to stand opposite the lady so that she might see her expressions clearly.

"If it had not been so dark, then I am sure such a thing

would never have happened," Lady Clara was saying, her hands clasped at her heart as she sighed heavily. "I would never have been discovered by the Duke, would never have been pulled into his arms without warning."

A young lady near Isobella gasped, her eyes wide. "Is that what happened? He came out of the darkness and caught you?"

Lady Clara nodded. "It was precisely like that. I was standing with Lady Sara. We were talking together, saying that we should return when, to my great fright, someone caught my arm. The next moment, his arms were around me and his head lowered! Such was my fear, I closed my eyes in fright, twisting away from him as I cried for him to release me! How glad I am that Lady Sara was there for she too began to cry out." She sighed again. "Once he realized I was not alone, he ran from me. It was deeply alarming."

"I am sorry to hear that," another lady said, as a few others murmured along with her. "The Duke of Exeter should be heartily ashamed of himself for such an action!"

"You were in the gardens when he found you?" Lady Amelia asked. She had stepped a short distance away from Isobella so that it did not look as though they were both determined to question Lady Clara thoroughly. "Yourself and Lady Sara?"

Lady Clara lifted her chin. "Yes. We had walked a short distance into the darker part of the gardens. I foolishly thought that it would be lit by lamps a little further along the way, but it was not."

"Then might I ask how you knew it was the Duke?"

It was not Isobella who asked this, nor was it Lady Amelia. Instead, another young lady spoke up, though Isobella did not think that it was with the same hope as she herself had to discover the truth. Rather, it sounded simply like a general question.

Lady Clara blinked. "Why, it was clear enough for me to see it was him."

"You did say it was very dark, however," Isobella said, quickly, as Lady Clara turned her attention towards her. "How could you have seen his face?"

"Because he was so near to me," she said, quickly.

Lady Amelia glanced at Isobella and then looked back at Lady Clara. "You told us all only a few moments ago that his head was lowered towards you, that you closed your eyes and screamed," she said, frowning. "How could you have seen his face if your eyes were closed, if you were pulling from him?"

There came a moment's pause, and Isobella's heart leapt up with a sense of triumph. Lady Clara was either mistaken in her assessment that it had been the Duke of Exeter, *or* she was lying.

"I recognized his voice." Lady Clara sniffed and then tossed her head. "I do not appreciate such questions, however. I know exactly what happened and – "

"Yet you must be absolutely sure it *was* the Duke of Exeter," Isobella said, breaking in. "To malign him without certainty puts you at great risk, Lady Clara."

Lady Clara's eyes rounded, color beginning to fade from her face. "Risk?"

"Of gossip," Lady Amelia said firmly. "There may be those who wonder why you spoke of the Duke without being entirely sure that it *was* he who did such a thing. If you are wrong, if you are mistaken, then there might well be consequences for such a thing. The *ton* would begin to speak of you instead of him."

Someone snorted, and near everyone in the group turned their heads to look.

"I am sure that Lady Clara knows *precisely* what it was that took place," said a young lady, her eyes flashing with the indignity of what both Amelia and Isobella had asked. "It is astonishing to me that two ladies of the *ton* would ask such questions when it is clear that Lady Clara is not only distressed but greatly upset by all that has occurred. Why would you do such a thing? Why would you not merely trust her words?"

The murmurings that went around the group told Isobella that she and Lady Amelia were not receiving the support of anyone. Undeterred, however, she returned the lady's sharp gaze with one of her own. "I am well aware of the difficulties that can arise from being spoken of in gossiping whispers as I am sure you are also," she said, firmly, drawing the attention of every young lady and gentleman present. "I will not engage in spreading any sort of gossip, but nor will I simply accept what is being said of someone without being certain that it is true. In this case, I am afraid that I cannot believe that the Duke of Exeter is as guilty as he is being purported to be, especially when he denies it."

The lady in question tutted and looked away from Isobella in seeming distain, given the way her lip curled. "How very disappointing. One would think that solidarity would be required from young ladies of the *ton*."

"There can and should be compassion, understanding, and shared sympathy with Lady Clara, I quite agree," Lady Amelia put in, before Isobella could respond. "That can still be offered even without believing that the Duke was responsible."

The lady in question – someone that Isobella did not

know by name – turned her sharp eyes towards Lady Amelia. "*I* was present that very evening. Lady Deborah and I spoke to the Duke before he stepped out into the darkness."

Bringing to mind all that the Duke had told them, Isobella recalled he had mentioned a Lady Victoria, assuming now that this was she. "He went further into the ground because he heard an exclamation," she said, again drawing the attention of everyone there, all of whom – save for Lady Victoria – had now lapsed into silence. "That has been verified by others, Lady Victoria." A hint of a smile brushed her lips as Lady Victoria started, perhaps surprised that Isobella knew of her title without having had a formal introduction. Or, mayhap, she did not much like that Isobella could speak so certainly of what had taken place that evening.

"So he stepped into the darkness, hearing someone else in distress," Lady Amelia added, tilting her head and lifting one eyebrow in Lady Victoria's direction. "And yet, somehow, *he* was the one who came upon Lady Clara in such a way? I do wonder if, somehow, there might have been some confusion there. It might well have been that there was someone else in the dark of the gardens that night."

Isobella took her gaze from Lady Victoria and returned it to Lady Clara. The lady was blinking rapidly, the color quite gone from her face now. Isobella held her breath but kept her expression outwardly calm, waiting for her to respond. The rest of the group waited too, each lady in turn, and each gentleman also directing their gaze towards her. Isobella's breathing grew shallower, waiting with desperate hope forming in her heart. Might there be something said at this very moment that would give the Duke even a light reprieve? Something that would permit him to hold his head high again?

"I – I suppose I cannot be *entirely* sure." Lady Clara looked down at her hands, then shrugged before, much to Isobella's interest, glancing at Lady Victoria. "All the same, however, I am certain I recognized his voice."

"It is always important in these matters to be quite certain," Lady Amelia said, only for Lady Victoria to take a step closer to Lady Clara, her finger pointing out towards her.

"Recall that you had Lady Sara with you," she said, in an almost commanding tone. "If we were to ask your friend about what took place, I am sure she would verify all that you have said about the Duke."

"Mayhap she would," Isobella replied, loudly enough to cover over everything that Lady Clara might say in response, "but the situation would be the same, Lady Victoria. It was terribly dark, there was a lot of commotion, and thus, the identification of the Duke might have been a mistake." Praying that the others around her would listen, she spread out her hands. "That, I have to say, is not good enough for me. Therefore, I will *not* believe that the Duke of Exeter was responsible for this until it is certain."

"Nor I," Lady Amelia said, confidently. "Thank you, Lady Clara, for expressing your doubts so honestly. You should have pride in that." She smiled warmly, and Lady Clara, after a moment, offered a tiny smile back in response. "Do excuse me."

Isobella watched as Lady Amelia stepped away and, waiting for only a few moments, then followed. Lady Victoria was red-faced, glaring at Lady Amelia as if she had said something deeply upsetting to her personally. Quite why she should be so affronted, Isobella did not understand, but nor did she care.

"That went marvelously!" Lady Amelia beamed at Isobella once she had caught up with her, her eyes shining.

"It most certainly did," Isobella agreed, taking her friend's arm as they walked across the park. "It may be that the Duke will feel able to stand up in society once more, even if there are many who will still doubt him."

Lady Amelia nodded. "That is something, at least. I must say, however, I was surprised at Lady Victoria's vehemence."

Considering this, Isobella nodded slowly. "Indeed, it was quite fervent, was it not?"

"Might it mean something?"

"We shall have to ask the Duke just what he knows of the lady," Isobella replied, frowning. "There might be a connection there, in some way."

"Or a connection between Lady Clara and Lady Victoria. If she is her cousin or some such thing, then it makes sense that she would wish to come to her defense."

"Agreed." With a sense of relief and hope beginning to build up in her heart, Isobella's steps grew lighter. "I am already looking forward to telling the Duke all that we have managed to achieve. I hope it will bring him some relief, at the very least."

Lady Amelia chuckled. "I am certain it will bring him a good deal more than that, Isobella."

Isobella flushed but did not reply, aware that the urgency to speak with the Duke was not solely because of what she might be able to share with him. All the same, she did not acknowledge it, letting it sit upon her heart but doing nothing with it. To trust him with her heart would be a great step indeed, and Isobella was not certain she was willing even to consider it. It would mean trusting again, believing his words, and holding them tightly to her. It would mean risking great pain, potential heartbreak, and a sorrow that would permeate to her very bones – and Isobella was not certain she had the strength to even think about doing so.

Perhaps remaining a spinster would be the best course of action after all.

Chapter Fourteen

Amos bowed his head. "Thank you for letting me come to call upon you, Lady Isobella."

The lady in question smiled back at him before gesturing for him to come and join her. Lady Amelia, he noted, was also present. That did not dissatisfy him in the least, although he had to admit a slight nudge of disappointment that he would not get to be solely in Lady Isobella's presence.

"It is good to see you both again," he said, sitting down in a seat that was directly opposite Lady Isobella. "These were not the circumstances I wanted to call upon you, Lady Isobella, but I am grateful to be here nonetheless."

A dusting of pink came into her cheeks, but she did not look away from him. "It is good that you have come, Your Grace. We have some news for you."

His eyebrows lifted. "So soon?"

"We had an... interesting conversation with Lady Clara yesterday afternoon," Lady Amelia told him, as the door opened and the tea tray was brought in. "Lady Isobella and I went to speak with her, and Miss Trentworth went in search of Lady Sara. She was the one who supposedly confirmed that it was you who attacked Lady Clara."

Amos swallowed hard, hating even the sound of those words being spoken aloud. "I see."

"It was in the midst of the fashionable hour, so there were quite a number of gentlemen and ladies present," Lady Isobella continued, rising to her feet to pour the tea. "Lady Clara was busy speaking of what had occurred, and we were able to ask some specific questions as regards what she had witnessed and endured."

"Oh." Amos licked his lips, nervousness capturing him. "She is quite convinced that it was I, I think."

Lady Amelia and Lady Isobella looked at each other, only for Lady Amelia to smile. "I do not think that she was as confident once we had reached the end of our conversation. The others there with us – various gentlemen and ladies – were listening most intently also."

Blinking quickly, Amos tried to take in what they were saying. "You – you are suggesting that there might have been a change of opinion in some of those present?"

"That is precisely what I am saying," Lady Isobella said, setting down a teacup in front of him and then smiling down into his eyes, making his heart leap. "Lady Clara could not make sense of what she said, I think, once we questioned her. How could it have been dark and yet she saw your face clearly?"

Unable to help himself, Amos reached out and caught her hand. "How can I thank you?"

Lady Isobella's eyes widened, only for her to smile and then gently tug her hand away. "We have not solved anything yet, Your Grace."

"You have sown doubt! That is enough."

"It may not be," Lady Amelia replied, reaching for her

teacup. "Recall, there are rumors about your poverty and the like. There may well be someone eager to continue with these rumors, even if Lady Clara's words are proven to be a little less than trustworthy."

His heart settled in his chest, no longer flooded with hope. "I see."

"But it is enough to start with," Lady Isobella added, perhaps seeing his sudden rise and then fall of hope and relief. "Strangely enough, there was another lady there who seemed quite determined to prove Lady Clara correct. A Lady Victoria? You mentioned her, I think."

"Yes, I did." A little concerned, Amos frowned. "You mean to say that she was defending Lady Clara? That she wished for you all to trust her words without hesitation?"

"Yes, precisely." Lady Isobella shrugged. "It seemed a little strange to me, for she was the one you had been speaking with, was she not? She and Lady Deborah. She saw you stepping away from them and going a little further into the gardens."

Amos nodded. "Yes, that is so. She heard the noise, I am sure, for she wanted me to make certain all was well. It was Lady Deborah who seemed to think nothing of it."

"We did question her on that," Lady Amelia said, setting her teacup down. "She could not deny it, especially when Isobella said that someone else had been able to verify that this was what had taken place."

Lady Isobella laughed softly. "I did not say who it was, of course. But it was enough for Lady Victoria to hesitate and that, in turn, led Lady Clara to admit that she might have made a mistake in identifying you – though she was loathe to say more than that."

Taking in a breath, Amos looked down at the table in front of him, taking his gaze from Lady Isobella so he would not become distracted. He was a little overawed by how much she and the other bluestockings had managed to achieve thus far for him, but at the same time, confused as to why Lady Victoria had been so vehement in her defense of Lady Clara.

"I cannot understand why Lady Victoria would be so determined," he said, looking down at the table still as his thoughts continued to come quickly, one after the other. "There must be a reason for it."

"I wondered how much you knew of her," Lady Isobella asked, as Amos lifted his head to look back at her. "Is she related in some way to Lady Clara?"

Amos frowned. "I do not know. It has never been mentioned, but I do not know the lady well." His eyebrows lifted. "I could ask Lord Galbraith. He is acquainted with Lord Welton – as am I, of course, but the gentleman might not wish to speak with me." Wincing, he managed a wry smile. "Lord Welton was not particularly favorable towards me the last time we conversed. I cannot imagine he will be any more so now!"

Lady Amelia frowned. "What does Lord Welton have to do with this?"

"He is a cousin of Lady Victoria."

"Oh." Lady Isobella looked to Lady Amelia, who gave a small shake of her head. "I did not know that. Well, if Lord Galbraith were able to find out if there is a connection, that would be helpful."

Amos hesitated, a question on his lips. "And... if there is not?"

Lady Isobella took a sip of her tea before she answered, a line drawing itself between her eyebrows. "Then we would have to consider what other reason there might be for her determination to prove Lady Clara correct."

With a slow nod, Amos drank the rest of his tea as they all sat in silence for a few minutes, each mind heavy with the weight of their thoughts. Amos set his china cup down, then let his gaze drift once more to Lady Isobella. She had not stopped frowning, her gaze somewhere on the wall behind him, but her expression was one of thoughtfulness. He had never expected her to be able to do something so quickly to help him and found himself a little in awe of just how much she had managed to do. It would have taken courage, he realized, to speak up against Lady Clara in amongst so many other ladies and gentlemen of the *ton*. There might well be those within the crowd who now thought badly of both herself and Lady Amelia for speaking and questioning as they had done, and that had all been on his account. A sudden guilt crashed into his heart, and he frowned.

"I am sorry if your willingness to help me has led to some in the *ton* thinking poorly of you for your refusal to believe Lady Clara without hesitation," he said, only for Lady Isobella to hold up one hand, palm out to him.

"Please, do not concern yourself in any way," she said, with a warm smile that spread light and relief into Amos' heart. "We are bluestockings, after all. We are well used to the *ton* thinking a little less of us!"

"Quite," Lady Amelia added with a smile of her own. "We are glad to be of help, Your Grace, truly."

Amos rose to his feet, then bowed low, wishing that he could take Lady Isobella's hand in his own again. "I am more than grateful," he said, meaning every word. "If there is anything I can do that would be of use, then please do tell me what it is."

"You can continue in society just as usual," Lady Isobella told him, as she too got to her feet. "You must not hide away, you must not make it appear as if you are guilty in any way."

Nodding, Amos felt a kick of nervousness in his stomach. "Some may give me the cut direct."

"Yes, they might." Lady Amelia lifted her shoulders and let them fall. "That cannot be helped."

"There will be those who will stand up with you all the same, however," Lady Isobella said, a light in her eyes that made Amos smile. "I am quite sure, especially after our conversation with Lady Clara, that there will be many in the *ton* who will not reject your company."

Pressing his lips flat for just a moment, Amos held Lady Isobella's gaze, the nervousness in his stomach growing swiftly. "Then might I hope you would be willing to stand up with me this evening, Lady Isobella?"

"To dance?"

He gave her a small nod, holding his breath now in anticipation.

"But of course." The happiness in her voice and the smile on her face brought him such great relief; his breath came out in a rush, forcing him to cover his embarrassment by bowing low again.

"I thank you. Lady Amelia, might you do me the honor also?"

The lady chuckled softly. "Your Grace, I am sure every bluestocking will dance with you, if you should ask us." Her eyes twinkled. "You are not going to be alone, I can assure you of that."

"Then I am already looking forward to this evening," he said, with more confidence than he truly felt as the nervous kick in his stomach returned. "Thank you. Thank you both. I feel as if there is a little light in this otherwise dark situation – and that is solely because of you."

Chapter Fifteen

Dancing with the Duke was not a new experience, but for Isobella, every moment felt tinged with excitement – an excitement that she tried hard to push down. She could not let herself feel anything for him, she reminded herself. It was much too dangerous to do so. Trust was not something she would give easily, if at all, and even though the Duke appeared to be quite trustworthy and genuine, had she not thought that before of the others?

"You are a little tense, I think."

Surprised, she looked up at the Duke, her breath hitching at just how close he was to her.

"You are not smiling either, which makes me fear you have too many things on your mind."

"I confess that I am a little distracted." Refusing to say as to why, she let him assume it was because of his present difficulties. "But I am enjoying our dance."

The smile on his face brought glimmers of gold to his eyes, and that, in turn, sent a light shiver down Isobella's spine. Heat infused her cheeks, praying silently that he had not felt it.

"As am I."

Those three words made the warmth in Isobella's face rush down to her core, the gentle way they were spoken whispering to her that there was more to it than a mere acknowledgement of the dance itself.

"I hope that the other dances have been just as enjoyable," she said quickly, spinning away from him for a moment before returning. "You have danced with all of my friends, I think." Fully aware that she was saying such a thing to deflect attention from their own connection, she flushed hot all over again at the knowing smile on his face.

"I have been very pleased with each and every dance thus far, yes," he acknowledged, taking her hand in his. "But this one, I think, is my favorite so far."

Isobella did not know what to say to that. There was so much he was offering her in that statement, so much that she dared not move forward to claim for herself. Could she tell him about her decision to remain a spinster? Should she do so? Might that push him away from this gentle pursuit of her?

"Alas, now we must part." With a light smile, the Duke released her and then stepped back, bowing as he did so. Isobella, curtsying quickly, was then offered his arm and, having no reason to refuse him, took it.

"Thank you for standing up with me," the Duke said, as he brought her back to where her friends were waiting. "I do hope we will be able to dance together again soon."

"As do I."

The words came from her without even a momentary thought about whether or not she should say them. It felt as if she was curling up slowly from the inside with mortification, her heart having betrayed her without her awareness. Out of the corner of her eye, she saw the Duke's head turn towards her, but could not bring herself to catch his eye. Why had she been so foolish in speaking so?

"I did not realize you were to stand up with the Duke of Exeter, sister. I saw you dancing with Lord Preston, but I did not think you would take the arm of the Duke of Exeter!"

Isobella blinked quickly, a little surprised to see her brother emerging out of the crowd to come and stand in front of them both. He was usually very good at permitting her to dance with whomever she wished – if she wished to dance at all – and whilst he stayed near, he did not ever intervene. "Granville, I did not think – "

"I apologize if there is some difficulty here, Lord Granville." The Duke dropped his arm so that Isobella was released from him, then inclined his head. "Forgive me, I should have been a little more considerate."

Isobella looked into her brother's face, seeing how he frowned as he studied the Duke's face, his lips thin and flat. Fear began to work its way into her heart, sending nervous tingles all the way down her arms. "Granville, there is nothing wrong, I assure you. I was glad to stand up with the Duke."

"Even though he is a scoundrel of the highest order?" Lord Granville took a step closer to the Duke, his voice mercifully low. "I have heard what you did to Lady Clara. I cannot imagine why you would then think it appropriate to dance with my sister!"

"Except I did no such thing," the Duke replied, calmly, looking straight into Lord Granville's eyes. "She mistook whoever it was for me. But I can understand your upset." Giving Isobella a small smile – one that did not hide the dark shadows that had leapt into his eyes – he took a step back from them both. "I shall take my leave of you now. Good evening."

Isobella waited for only a moment before rounding on her brother, her upset increasing with every second. "How could you do such a thing?"

"How could *you* be so foolish?" her brother asked, just as Louisa came to join them both, her eyes darting between one and the other. "Do you not know what is being said of him?"

Isobella drew herself up, a cold anger taking hold of her. "I did not think that you were someone who believed gossip, Granville." She held his gaze without blinking, silently reminding him of all that had occurred in her past, of all the times that society had whispered about *her* even though she had done nothing to merit it.

"I am afraid your sister has a point, my love." Louisa set a hand on her husband's arm, but he did not look away from Isobella. "You have always trusted her judgment, have you not? Why should you change now?"

"Because I cannot bear to have you injured yet again!" Speaking in answer to his wife's question, he spoke directly to Isobella. "You have already endured so much, Isobella. What if this Duke is yet another blight upon your life?"

Awash with a sudden gratitude, Isobella reached to take her brother's hand. "You are concerned for me because of his reputation, yes?"

He nodded, his shoulders slumping just a little.

"But I do not believe the gossip," Isobella told him, gently but firmly. "I will not accept it as the truth, not until I know for certain."

"The rumors must have some basis in truth, however," he stated, looking at her askance. "They have been speaking of his lack of fortune!"

"Untrue." Her head lifted. "What else?"

"He is a gambler, a gentleman who seeks out places of disrepute."

Isobella shook her head. "You could speak to his sister and to his brother-in-law, Lord Galbraith. They would say that is false."

Her brother twisted his lips. "What of the murmur that his estate is in a state of disrepair? That he will not permit anyone to come to call because it is so utterly dreadful."

Having not heard of such a thing before, Isobella did not give them more than a single thought. "I am quite certain that is nothing more than a rumor, idle gossip seeking to bring him down."

"Lady Clara has told us all," he countered, still determined, evidently still unwilling to give up all of his concern at once. "She told us clearly that – "

"Except I heard that she was not as sure as she first made out," Louisa interrupted, wincing when her husband shot her a sharp look. "She was in conversation recently and had to admit that she had not seen the gentleman's face. I believe she stated that she was still sure but could not be entirely certain that it was he."

Isobella watched her brother carefully, seeing him take in a long breath and then close his eyes as he exhaled.

"I do not want to be the one to take you away from this chance of happiness," he said, slowly, opening his eyes to look at her. "But I am afraid for you, Isobella."

She smiled at him softly. "There is nothing to be concerned about, I assure you. I am grateful for your concern; however, I trust that the Duke of Exeter has an excellent character."

Her brother's eyes widened at the corners as he took a

step closer to her. "Do you mean to say that you have come to care for him?"

Isobella rebuffed this at once, her heart throwing itself into a furious rhythm. "No, not in the least! I would never permit myself to – "

"I do not think that now is the time for such a discussion." Louisa put a hand on her husband's arm, throwing a smile at Isobella. "Besides which, I think there may be others vying for the Duke's attention, and we should not begin to hope for anything that might not be."

"I am not hoping at all," Isobella said firmly, ignoring the cry of her heart. "I just refuse to accept what is said of someone, that is all."

Lord Granville ducked his head, looking a little embarrassed. "I shall have to go to speak with the Duke now, will I not?"

"Yes, I think you shall." With a chuckle, Louisa took Isobella's arm and then turned away directly, leaving her husband to go in search of the Duke. "Now, Isobella, I am not going to question you as regards the Duke himself, but I must warn you to be careful. I should not like to see you hurt again."

Isobella's heart thudded wildly. "I have no thoughts as regards the Duke, Louisa, truly."

Her sister in law did not disagree with her but only smiled. "Be that as it may, just be aware that there are those in society who are... or who *were* hopeful of another match."

"Might I ask with whom?" Isobella could not help her curiosity, a knot twisting in her stomach. "Is it someone I am acquainted with?"

"I do not know if you are acquainted with Lady Deborah," Louisa told her, sending a sidelong glance in Isobella's direction. "Although I have heard she is a lady with a good many suitors – or gentlemen who would wish to be suitors, at least! There may be no connection between them any longer now, since there are these whispers about him." Her lips twisted. "When a young lady has good standing, beauty, and an outstanding dowry, is it any wonder that she has so many gentlemen pursuing her? She will not care if the Duke is no longer available, I am sure."

The knot in Isobella's stomach grew tighter. "I see."

"But given that you are not in the least bit interested in the Duke, it should not concern you, should it?" Louisa smiled, but Isobella did not respond, fully aware that what she had said to her sister in law and what she truly felt were quite at odds with each other. Instead, all she gave Louisa was a smile, saying nothing more, and soon Louisa changed the subject to something a good deal more banal. All the while, however, Isobella's thoughts lingered on the Duke of Exeter, wondering if there might be a connection between himself and Lady Deborah after all... and thereafter, why her heart felt so terribly painful at even the thought of it all.

Chapter Sixteen

"I have found no connection between Lady Clara and Lady Victoria." Amos looked straight down into Lady Isobella's eyes, seeing how her lips pursed with displeasure as they stood outside on the busy London street. "Lord Galbraith has been very discreet with his questions, but he did not find anything of use. It seems that although they are acquainted, they are not related."

"Thank you for your endeavors." With a sigh, she turned around and then made her way towards the door of the library. They had arranged to meet for a brief conversation in public, but now Amos could think of nothing other than being in her company. "I am also sorry to hear of the other rumors spread about you."

This made Amos' eyebrows lift high. "New rumors?"

Twisting her head around to look at him, Lady Isobella's cheeks grew rosy as she turned to face him. "You have not heard? My brother was the one who informed me of it."

Amos frowned. "He did come to apologize to me."

"Oh, not that he believes it, of course!" Lady Isobella put her hand on his arm, her eyes searching his, and the urge to lower his head became so strong, Amos had to squeeze his hand into a fist so that his fingernails bit hard into his palms. "It was evidently some whisper that your estate is in a state of disrepair."

He flushed hot. "It most certainly is not!"

"I believe you," she said, holding her hand to his arm still. "My brother does also, albeit after some discussion." Her lips curved into a gentle smile, and then she took her hand away. "But there is someone who has begun to speak of you, that is quite certain."

"Lady Clara?"

Lady Isobella shook her head. "I do not think it would have been her. Her fear did seem real, and I am sure that she experienced this dreadful thing that happened to her, but I do *not* think it was you. Someone convinced her that it was you, however. I am quite certain of that."

"Most likely, Lady Sara?"

She hesitated. "Mayhap. Or Lady Victoria, given her determination to have us all believe the lady. The vehemence Lady Victoria displayed was quite extraordinary, and my heart tells me that there is something more to it than just mere friendship... if there was even that between them!" Her head tilted towards the door of the library. "Do you wish to join us, or is there somewhere else you need to be?"

Amos could not have been held back. "But of course." Following her into the library, he looked all around him, glad to still be lingering in conversation with Lady Isobella. It was not in the least bit quiet, much to his surprise. There were conversations going on in many parts of the establishment, with some visitors seeming to be there solely for conversation!

"You have not been in here before?"

"I have but not in many years," Amos replied, looking all around him as, to his delight, Lady Isobella took his arm so they might walk together. "It has become a little more of a social gathering than I remembered."

Lady Isobella screwed up her face. "Indeed, it has been. I wish it were not so, but all the same, I am glad to be surrounded by so many books." Her smile returned. "There is so much here, so much just waiting to be read and learned and explored. I feel the happiest when I am within a place like this."

Amos slowed his steps, taking her in as she spoke. There was a beauty about her unlike anything he had ever seen before, something so incredible, it stole his breath away. It was as if, upon stepping into the library, she had come alive in a new, fresh way. There was almost a glow about her hazel eyes, the tiny, delicate smile lifting the corners of her lips a testament to just how happy this place made her. The way she clasped her hands at her heart and sighed content-edly made his own heart sing, delighting in the happiness that this place brought to her.

"Forgive me." Catching his eye and, no doubt, the way that he was looking at her, Lady Isobella blushed red. "I was distracted."

"It is quite all right. It is a delight for me to see just how much this place means to you."

She dropped her gaze to the floor for a moment. "It does bring me joy, certainly. But," she took a deep breath and set her shoulders, "there is work to be done." Glancing about her, she looked at the other bluestockings. "We are all going to be searching for information about the ladies – and their families – involved in this situation. It may very well come to naught since you have told me that Lady Clara and Lady Victoria have no connection between them – but all the same, the bluestockings and I agree it would be worth making certain of it. Besides which," she finished, with a quiet sigh, "there is not very much else we can do at present."

"I am grateful for all the help you and the other bluestockings have offered me thus far," Amos said, wanting her to know just how thankful he was. "It might seem like very little to you, but it means a great deal to me. Already, what you have done and said has made a difference."

"Ah, but we are always determined to get to the truth, no matter how long it may take us," Lady Isobella answered, still walking beside him, her hand on his arm still. "We will find out who is whispering about you, Your Grace. I am sure of it."

Amos said nothing, taking great pleasure in having the lady on his arm. There was something quite delightful about having her beside him, walking together as though they were simply out to enjoy one another's company.

"Now, it is here I must begin my search." Lady Isobella gestured to a row of books. "If you will excuse me?"

Disappointed that he was unable to linger beside her, Amos stepped back and watched as she walked away from him, towards this row of books. He continued to study her as she took out one book and then, setting it on a small table, began to look through it. Quite what it was she was looking for, Amos did not know, but he was quite content to wait for her to finish her study.

"Your Grace. I must say, I am astonished to see you here."

He turned quickly, not wanting anyone to see him studying Lady Isobella with such intensity. "Good afternoon." Bowing quickly, he lifted his head and looked straight back into the eyes of Lady Deborah. Surprise lurched through his heart as the lady's eyebrow arched.

"As I have said, I am astonished to see you making your way through London as if there is nothing is being said of you."

Uncertain as to what he ought to say or why she was making such a remark, Amos hesitated. "I – I will not permit the *ton* to whisper about me and force me to hide away because of it."

"I see." She did not say whether or not she believed this about him, and that unsettled Amos somewhat. "But you will, it seems, bring Lady Isobella's reputation into question by walking in and speaking with her?"

It was a strange question, and Amos, uncertain of what to make of it, did not immediately answer. The silence lingered between them both but still, he waited, wondering what Lady Deborah meant by such a statement. Was she concerned for Lady Isobella? Or surprised at Lady Isobella's willingness to come alongside him?

"She is a bluestocking, I suppose." Lady Deborah sighed and rolled her eyes. "I suppose that it would not be of any real concern to *her* what the *ton* has to say? She will be dealing with more than enough whispers about her bluestocking ways already."

"I would not be speaking to Lady Isobella if she did not wish me to," he said, disliking Lady Deborah's tone. "But I thank you for your concern."

"Whatever are you doing speaking with *him*?"

Amos took a step back, his irritation now growing to anger as a gentleman came to stand directly beside Lady Deborah, his jaw tight. "Lord Welton, good afternoon."

The gentleman's lip curled. "I do not think I was speaking to you, Your Grace."

Affronted, Amos made to respond only to snap his mouth closed. He did not want to make things worse. It would be best for him to step away.

"I can speak to whomever I wish, Lord Welton." Lady Deborah's voice grew higher in pitch, her eyes sharpening. "You have no reason to come to interrupt me."

Amos held up both hands. "If you will excuse me." Aware that there were others in the room turning to look at him, he made to step away, but Lady Deborah interrupted him.

"There is no need, Your Grace. I can assure you that I am well able to make my own decisions in such things."

"But you are showing no wisdom!" Lord Welton exclaimed, surprising Amos with just how forward he was to speak to the lady in such a way. "Do you not know of all that has been said of the Duke of Exeter?"

He is speaking as if I am not present. Drawing himself up, Amos lifted his chin high. "There is much that has been said, Lord Welton, but none of it is true."

Lord Welton scoffed loudly. "Of *course* you would say such a thing, Your Grace, but we all know what you did at the ball."

Wanting to deny it, Amos drew himself up. "There has been a mistake. It was not I who did such a thing. I am sorry it happened to Lady Clara, but I can assure you – "

"I do not know why we are even *listening* to you." Dismissing him, Lord Welton turned around so that his back was to Amos. "Lady Deborah, might I remind you that – "

"There is *nothing* between us, Lord Welton. No matter what your family expects, I have made my decision clear!"

Those words made Amos' astonishment overtake his anger. He had never thought that Lady Deborah might be in any way connected to Lord Welton! Evidently, however, it seemed that Lord Welton very much wished for there to be, that there was an expectation that she was choosing to step back from. How many others were aware of this?

"Lady Deborah, might I ask you for your opinion on this?" Lady Isobella, who had been only a short distance away, came towards Lady Deborah, a book in her hand. She was smiling warmly, and her tone was light, shattering the tension between them all.

Lady Deborah blinked, then looked down at the book Lady Isobella was holding. "What is it you should like to ask me?"

Amos could not help but smile, despite the difficult situation. Lady Isobella had acted quickly and calmly, diffusing the upset and had come instead to distract Lady Deborah whilst pulling her away from Lord Welton. He returned his gaze to Lord Welton, turning his head as he did so, only for a sharp pain to crack across his cheek and nose.

He heard cries of astonishment, of fright, mayhap, as he staggered back, slamming into a stacked bookshelf. Pain tore through his head as he fought to regain his standing, trying to understand what it was that had just happened to him.

"You struck the Duke of Exeter?" he heard someone cry, as he rubbed one hand over his eyes, his vision blurred. "Why ever should you do such a thing?"

"Because he deserved it," Amos heard Lord Welton shout as he stood up tall, his fingers now running over his jaw. "Mayhap now you will realize the danger you are in when you stay in his company!"

Shame burnt into Amos's soul as he glanced around the room and saw every eye on him. This was not his fault, not his doing, but at the same time, having everyone looking at him with a mixture of disdain and shock upon their faces made him feel as though he deserved every dark look. Without another word, without another look towards Lady Isobella, Amos made his way directly out of the library, heat swirling into his chest and core. Keeping his head down, his jaw still aching, he made his way directly back towards his carriage, his heart beating furiously. Despite all Lady Isobella had done, despite her attempts to help him thus far and even in taking Lady Deborah away from the conversation, it had not been enough. He had been mortified and shamed all over again and feared now that society would whisper about him all the more.

Just what was he to do?

Chapter Seventeen

"Whatever was Lord Welton doing?"

Isobella shook her head and then reached for her teacup. "I do not know." Recalling what had happened the previous afternoon, she took a sip of her tea, her brow furrowing. "Lord Welton was quite determined to prevent Lady Deborah from speaking with the Duke. I went to speak with Lady Deborah to take her away from the conversation, for more than a few people were looking over. Then, as she and I stepped away, Lord Welton planted the Duke a facer! It was an awful thing to witness."

"But without any real explanation?"

Isobella bit her lip. "I do recall him shouting to Lady Deborah thereafter that he was doing so because the Duke deserved it. It was certainly a very strong reaction." *And the Duke left immediately thereafter,* she thought to herself, wishing he had not run from the library as he had done. They had not spoken since then, and whilst she had felt the urge to write to him, to send a note to make certain he was quite well, she had not done so. It would betray her heart too much, she feared.

"An overreaction, one might say," Miss Trentworth suggested as the other bluestockings murmured their agreement. "And none of us discovered anything of interest during our search?"

Looking all around the room, Isobella's heart sank as the other bluestockings all shook their heads. The library had been filled with history books, all detailing the various families of the aristocracy. Each of them had searched for something, some sort of connection that might connect Lady Victoria to Lady Clara, Lady Clara to Lady Sara, or Lady Sara to Lady Victoria in some way, but it seemed that none of them had found anything of note. That was a little troubling, for it felt as though they were walking through clouds, having no certainty about where to put their next step.

"Lady Sara's family is all quite respectable. None of them has any connection to Lady Clara, however." Lady Amelia spread out her hands. "I wish there was something more to share with you than that, but there is not."

"And the same is to be said of Lady Victoria." Lady Rosalyn winced at Isobella's sharp look. "Again, I wish that there had been something that caught our attention, but there was nothing."

"*Someone* must have convinced Lady Clara that the Duke of Exeter was the one who had attacked her that night." Rubbing her hand over her eyes, Isobella's heart twisted. "Whoever it was had a reason for it. But now neither Lady Sara nor Lady Victoria has any connection to Lady Clara or to the Duke himself! There is no great friendship between any of these ladies, either. So why was Lady Victoria so very determined to have all of us believe Lady Clara without hesitation?"

And what does our lack of success mean for the Duke?
Amelia closed her eyes and winced as the memory of him
falling back into a bookcase, the pain tearing into his expression, ran through her mind. She had taken a step closer,
ready to go to him, but he had turned sharply and run from
the library, his shoulders hunched and his head bowed. Was
that how he was to be from now on? Ashamed, hiding away,
vilified by those who believed lies about him?

A thought suddenly came to her, her breath hitching.
"What if Lord Welton is the one whispering rumors about
the Duke?"

A few seconds of silence answered her, and for a
moment, Isobella feared that she might well be mistaken in
her thoughts. Then, however, Lady Amelia began to nod.

"We had not thought of him before, I know, but it
would make sense, would it not? Perhaps we have been
looking in the wrong direction!"

"It would make sense, yes, given that he has been so
very fervent in his dislike of the Duke," Miss Sherwood
agreed, her eyes darting from one to another. "Did not the
Duke say that he did not feel Lord Welton particularly
warm towards him even before all of this?"

Isobella took another sip of her tea and then set her cup
down. "If we suspect that it might be him, surely we must
then also think that *he* was the one who, somehow, encouraged Lady Clara to think that it was the Duke who attacked
her in the gardens that evening?"

"It could be so," Lady Rosalyn agreed, sounding a little
more excited now. "It would be understandable for it all to
be the same person."

"But why?" Isobella, leaning forward in her chair,
searched every face. "Why would he do such a thing? What
motivation does he have?"

Miss Trentworth frowned. "I do not know. I am not even acquainted with the gentleman, so I cannot even imagine what motivation he might have."

"The Duke might have some thoughts on that matter?" Lady Amelia's question sounded innocent enough, but the glimmer in her eye was not something Isobella missed. She frowned, then flushed, wondering if the other bluestockings understood what such a look might mean.

"It would be wise to ask him," Lady Rosalyn agreed. "Might you discuss it with him?"

"And we have not looked into the family of Lord Welton as yet either, have we?" Miss Sherwood continued, as Isobella nodded in answer to Lady Rosalyn's question. "Might there be something we can discover from his family history that would connect him to Lady Clara?"

"Or to the Duke himself?" Miss Trentworth suggested. "It would be worth ascertaining, yes."

Every eye turned towards Isobella, and although she had already nodded in agreement with what Lady Amelia had asked her, she did so again. "Yes, I can speak with the Duke of Exeter and ask him if there is any connection between himself and Lord Welton and if he knows why Lord Welton seems to dislike him so." A flurry of anticipation writhed in her stomach, but Isobella did her best not to let it show in her expression. Nor did she let herself linger on such a feeling, fully aware as to why she felt such a way. The Duke was becoming more and more important to her and try as she might, she could not pretend she felt nothing for him.

I must find the truth first, she thought to herself. *Thereafter, there might be time for such thoughts.*

"When will you speak with the Duke?" Miss Sherwood wanted to know. "Soon?"

"This evening, mayhap," Isobella answered. "Lord Gallagher's ball is this evening, and I have heard it is one of the most sought-after invitations of the Season."

Lady Rosalyn laughed softly. "It most certainly is. I confess, I am very eager indeed to attend, for I have heard there will be all manner of entertainments as well as dancing!"

Isobella smiled but had to admit that the thought of such a thing was not particularly exciting for her. The only thing that brought a little anticipation to her heart was the thought of seeing the Duke again, and that, she hoped, would be very soon indeed.

"Might I say that you look quite enchanting this evening, Lady Isobella?"

"I thank you." Isobella gave a smile to Lord Preston but inwardly wished that he would soon step away. The gentleman was nothing if not persistent, nearly dogging her since his arrival at the ball when he had discovered her standing at the side of the room, near to the other bluestockings. "I am sure that – "

"Did you hear what Lord Welton did to the Duke of Exeter?" Lord Preston interrupted, speaking in much too loud a voice for Isobella's liking. "The Duke was speaking *most* disagreeably about Lady Deborah, and Lord Welton called him out! When the Duke continued to insult her, Lord Welton had no choice but to defend her – and himself, I believe."

Isobella narrowed her eyes, her jaw tight. "I beg your pardon?"

"It is all quite true!" Lord Preston exclaimed, looking back at her with slightly widened eyes. "I am sure you will not stand up with him this evening, Lady Isobella. You will not – must not – even speak with him, for – "

"I am astonished that you would believe such rumors, Lord Preston." Interrupting *him* this time, Isobella took a step closer to the gentleman, who immediately began to frown. "Why would you say such things about the Duke of Exeter?"

"Because Lord Welton told me himself!" Lord Preston exclaimed, sounding entirely genuine, but his words struck hard at Isobella. "He is a gentleman who can be trusted, and there were *many* others present who heard all that took place."

Isobella lifted her chin. "*I* was one of those present, Lord Preston. It was not at all as you have described."

The change that came over Lord Preston's face was quite astonishing. He went from wide-eyed and hopeful to uncertain and confused. His eyebrows lowered, his mouth opened and then closed again, and his eyes darted from one side to the other.

"I heard every word Lord Welton said to the Duke," she continued, speaking in a low voice so that only he could hear. "I can assure you, nothing like that was said. I shall bear testament to it if I have to. Now," she finished, angry with his presence and with his determination to believe all he had been told by others, "if you will excuse me, Lord Preston, I wish to go and find the very gentleman you think that I should not be speaking to." Stepping away, she battled with her upset and her frustration against all that Lord Preston had said of the Duke. This was the gentleman she cared for, the gentleman she was excited to see, the gentleman she *wanted* to be in company with. She felt almost indignant that Lord Preston would even dream of speaking about him in such a way!

Isobella stopped short, her eyes flaring, her breath catching in her chest. In her heart, in her mind, she had just admitted to herself that she cared for the Duke of Exeter, that her affections were very much engaged when it came to him. Did that mean she trusted him? That she was *willing* to trust him?

"Lady Isobella?"

A familiar voice, a welcome voice, caught her attention, and closing her eyes, she let out a slow breath and then turned towards the Duke. "Your Grace."

"Are you quite all right?"

The noise of the ballroom faded away as she looked up into his eyes, steadying herself there as her frustration and upset faded to nothing. "Yes, I am. I thank you." Letting out her breath slowly, she looked up at him. "Are *you* quite well?" Her gaze ran over his cheek and jaw, seeing the bruises there. "We have not spoken since Lord Welton injured you. I have been greatly concerned for you."

The Duke, much to her surprise, dropped his head and rubbed the back of his neck. Was he ashamed? Embarrassed? Compassion grew swiftly, and she moved a little closer, doing her best to be surreptitious for fear of someone near them looking over, but at the same time, doing her best to express how she felt. Her hand reached out, then pulled back, only for her to force herself to do what she felt she needed to.

She took his hand.

Fire ripped up her arm towards her heart as his head lifted, his eyes rounding.

"What happened was not your fault," she said, very quietly indeed. "In fact, I was hoping that you and I might speak on the matter? The bluestockings and I have had an idea about this entire situation."

The Duke said nothing, his gaze travelling down to their joined hands, and Isobella, flushing hot, pulled her hand away.

"Lord Welton," she continued, her voice catching a little, such was the plethora of emotions rushing through her. "What do you know of him?"

It took the Duke a few moments to respond, blinking quickly as if pulling himself out of a trace. "Lord Welton?" he repeated, before shrugging. "I know nothing about him. I was only just introduced to him some weeks ago."

This made Isobella frown. "Then there is no connection between yourself and his family?"

"None."

Flattening her lips, Isobella fought back at the frustration building in her again. She was the one who had come up with that thought, and now it felt like she was pushing herself back into the shadows.

"Although he is a cousin to Lady Victoria," the Duke continued, as Isobella's eyes flew open. "I told you that before, I am sure."

She blinked. "Yes, you did, but I had forgotten." Her fingers touched the Duke's hand again, clasping them tightly as thought after thought began to pour into her mind. "Then there must be a connection *there*, then! Lady Victoria was quite determined that we believe Lady Clara. Lord Welton is a cousin of hers, and he has always had a dislike of you."

The Duke began to nod slowly, not pulling his hand away but running his other hand across his chin. All the while, the noises of the ball went around them, but no one seemed in the least bit interested in their conversation.

"He said something, before he punched me." With a snatch of breath, he returned his gaze to Isobella, her heart lurching at the light in his eyes. "He was speaking to Lady Deborah, but she responded to him very harshly, stating that there was *nothing* between them, no matter what his family said. No connection or the like."

It was as if she were walking up a steep path, a hint of the sunrise before her. All she had to do was reach the top, and the light would be shining in its full glory, spreading out in front of her. "Lady Deborah is unwilling to pull towards Lord Welton but Lord Welton wishes it," she said, half to herself and half to him. "There might be something there, then. Something that we have not yet seen."

"A connection that *he* wants but she does not." The Duke pressed her fingers, leaning down towards her so he could speak quietly but with great fervency. "A connection that the family clearly expects but that she will not give."

"That does not give us a reason for Lady Clara's statement about you, however." Biting her lip, Isobella looked away from him. "But it is something, however. To discover why Lord Welton treated you so, why he has such a dislike of you, that will be pertinent, mayhap."

The Duke smiled gently. "You are taking great pains on my behalf, Lady Isobella. You and the other bluestockings. I cannot tell you how much I value it though, more than that, I value your trust in me."

Isobella gazed up into his eyes and found herself lost. She did not respond to what he had said, her thoughts coming to an instant stop. The green and gold in his eyes melded together, the swirl they created enchanting her.

"Lady Isobella." There was a huskiness about his voice that sent a tingling up her spine. "If I might be honest, I – "

"I cannot." She turned away from him sharply, beginning to stride blindly forward, aware of just how much she had longed to do, just how much she had wanted *him* to do.

Right there, in the ballroom, she had felt her heart begin to yearn for him, to long for him to bend his head and kiss her. Why was she so foolish? Why could she not keep control of her emotions? Why was she so willing to throw aside all that she had determined and lose herself in the eyes of the Duke?

"I did not mean to startle you." His hand reached out, caught her arm, and then dropped again as she turned to look at him, breathing hard. "Forgive me, Lady Isobella. Now is not the moment for any sort of discussion on matters of the heart... although I pray that you can tell just how much I have begun to care for you."

Isobella swallowed at the knot in her throat, trying to find the words to rebuff him, to push him away from her, but she could not. To say such a thing aloud would sever their connection, and for some reason, she could not bring herself to do so.

"But we must concentrate on the matter at hand, of course." When she did not respond, the Duke offered her a small smile, looking a little uncertain. "And such conversations should certainly not take place at a ball."

"Indeed not," she managed to say, glancing over the Duke's shoulder and seeing Lady Amelia looking at her with careful eyes, watching everything that was going on – no doubt to keep Isobella safe. "The rumors and the story with Lady Clara are the thing we ought to focus on at present."

He nodded, a redness growing in his face. "Of course. So, what must be done?"

Isobella took in a calming breath and then released it, allowing her heart to quieten as practicality took over. "I will return to the library and look for anything in there about Lord Welton's family line and their connection to

Lady Deborah. I shall have the other bluestockings ask quietly amongst their acquaintances also, and I might very well speak to Lady Deborah also."

He nodded. "And what can I do?"

"Keep your head held high," she answered, with what she hoped was an encouraging smile. "Believe that soon, we will have all the answers you need."

Chapter Eighteen

"I think I am in love with her, Galbraith." Amos swirled his whisky in the bottom of his glass and then looked at his brother-in-law. "I do not think I have ever felt such a way before."

Lord Galbraith smiled his understanding.

"I cannot bear to be away from her," Amos continued, looking away now. "She is intelligent, kind, gentle of heart, and nothing but beautiful. I do not wish only to court her now but to think of the future!"

This made Lord Galbraith's eyebrows lift. "Is that so?"

"It is," Amos continued, with a grimace, "I cannot tell how she feels about me. That is a little difficult." Remembering how she had twisted away from him when there had been a moment of importance growing between them, he shook his head. "When I asked if I could call on her some time ago, she did not answer in the affirmative. In fact, now that I think on it, I would say that she looked almost afraid."

"Of you calling to take tea?"

Amos nodded. "Yes. That is strange, I know, but I am sure that is what I saw in her expression."

"And so you dare not ask her again?" Lord Galbraith shook his head as Amos frowned. "Is that it?"

"There has not been an opportunity." With a sigh, Amos spread out his hands. "The rumors and the lies began soon after, and I did not have a chance to do so." His chest rose and then fell with a heavy breath. "Lord Granville himself did not appear to be particularly pleased with my desire to stand up with Lady Isobella either. Yes, he apologized for his remarks thereafter, but there was still concern there."

"As you can understand, I am sure."

Amos rolled his eyes. "I know, I know. A good gentleman should be worried about his sister and her prospects, wanting to shield her from the very worst of fellows, but I am *not* as society says!"

Lord Galbraith shrugged. "Then go and speak with him."

"With Lord Granville?"

His brother-in-law nodded. "Yes. Tell him of your intentions as regards Lady Isobella – only with her agreement, of course – and see if he would be willing to consider you. That way, you will be able to tell whether or not there is any hope."

A nervousness washed over Amos' frame. "I suppose I could do such a thing."

"Why would you hesitate?" Lord Galbraith's lips lifted in a light smile. "When I fell in love with your sister, nothing could keep me back from her. Nothing whatsoever." His head tilted to one side. "Does your heart not feel the same way?"

"It does, yes." There was no hesitation on Amos' part, aware of just how strongly he felt. With a nod, he got to his feet. "You are quite right. I *shall* go to speak with Lord Granville."

"Now?" Lord Galbraith's eyebrows shot towards his hairline. "So quickly?"

"Why not?" Amos chuckled as he walked to the door. "There is no reason for hesitancy, is there? Pray for my good fortune, brother!"

Bowing low, Amos tried to ignore the twist of uncertainty in his stomach. "Lord Granville, thank you for allowing me to call so unexpectedly."

The gentleman waved Amos to a chair, his smile a little hesitant. "But of course. Lady Isobella is not here at present, however."

"It is to you that I wished to speak," Amos replied, seeing the man's eyebrows lift. "I am aware that there has been some... uncertainty as to my good name, and I wanted to assure you that whilst there are many whispers about me, none of them are true."

Lord Granville cleared his throat, looking a little abashed. "Your Grace, I did apologize for my own foolish-ness in accusing you of all that society has thrown at you."

Amos waved one hand. "Of course, of course. It is... " The words began to stick in his throat, and he looked away, finding it easier to speak when he was not looking directly at Lord Granville. "I wish to know whether or not you would have any concerns if I were to pursue Lady Isobella."

Silence met him, and Amos returned his gaze to Lord Granville, seeing how the gentleman frowned. His heart began to sink.

"If there was hesitancy on your part, then I would

respect that," Amos added hastily. "I have said nothing to Lady Isobella as yet." *Although I have tried.*

Lord Granville rose to his feet and walked to the side of the room, pouring them both a drink. "I will be honest, Your Grace. There *is* some hesitancy there."

All of Amos' hopes crashed to the floor.

"But not on account of you," the gentleman continued, making Amos frown in confusion. "When I apologized to you, Your Grace, I meant it."

Taking the glass of brandy from him, Amos nodded his thanks. "I appreciate your trust in me, Lord Granville."

"It was brought about by both Isobella's conviction and my wife's also," the gentleman replied, sitting back down again. "As I have said, there is no concern on my part when it comes to your character, Your Grace. If Isobella trusts you, then I trust her judgment."

Amos smiled.

"But I must wonder if Isobella herself would willingly accept you," Lord Granville continued, sounding a trifle concerned. "To be clear, I hope that she would but... well, without going into detail, let me say that I felt she has an uncertainty there."

Taking a sip of his brandy, Amos considered his response. That was, he considered, all he had seen in Lady Isobella himself, had he not? The hope that had only just begun to rebuild itself immediately crashed to the floor again. "I can understand that concern."

"Oh?"

Amos gave him a wry smile. "I did ask if I might call on her some time ago. Her response was somewhat muted."

Lord Granville sighed and shook his head. "After I spoke to you at the ball, my wife decided to speak with me

about Isobella. She and I are both a little concerned for her."
He grimaced, then brought his brandy to his lips. "I am not
certain I should share all these things with you, Your Grace.
They are Isobella's past and Isobella's pain... but let me say
this." Sitting up a little straighter, he looked directly into
Amos' gaze. "Isobella has been deeply hurt by not only one
gentleman but three. The last was particularly painful, I am
afraid. Louisa – my wife – thinks that Isobella is too afraid
to let herself care for another again."

Pain struck at Amos' heart, though it was not pain for
himself. Instead, there was a deep sympathy in his heart for
her, wondering just how much she had been forced to
endure. "I am very sorry to hear that."

"She will tell you all, if she decides to do so," Lord
Granville continued, as Amos' heart began to ache all the
more. "So, in answer to your question, Your Grace, you most
certainly have my blessing should you decide to do so, but it
will be up to Isobella herself as to whether or not she
accepts."

"I understand." Amos finished his brandy and then
nodded to Lord Granville. "Thank you for speaking
with me."

Lord Granville got to his feet and then shook Amos's
hand firmly. "I do hope that she will accept you, Your
Grace. She is the most wonderful of sisters and deserves
happiness."

"I have every intention of giving her as much happiness
as I can, should she accept," Amos answered, aware that his
feelings towards the lady were coming out in his words but
caring nothing for that. "Thank you, Lord Granville."

The gentleman nodded, and Amos quit the room, his
head heavy with thoughts. Whatever had happened to

Lady Isobella, she bore the pain of it still. That was what held her back from accepting him, mayhap?

I must speak to her, he thought to himself, stepping out into his carriage. *I must be entirely honest with her, I must express my heart and hope that she will be willing to do the same.*

Chapter Nineteen

sobella frowned, tracing her finger along the lines written in the book. She had been in the busy London library with the other bluestockings for some time, but until this moment, had found nothing whatsoever related to Lord Welton.

Now, however, a few lines had changed everything. Lifting her head, she looked about for the others, spying Lady Amelia standing closest to her.

"Amelia." Beckoning to her friend, she waited until she drew nearer. "Look at this."

Reading the few lines, Lady Amelia's gasp made Isobella's confidence rise. She *had,* then, found something of significance.

"A family agreement?" Lady Amelia said, lifting her gaze from the book. "This is an age-old agreement, however, is it not?"

"It does appear to be." Isobella leaned closer to the book, screwing up her eyes just a little as she tried to read the words. "It appears to say that there should always be a familial connection between Welton and Hately... an agreement from of old between the two gentlemen bearing the titles at the time." Her head lifted. "Lady Deborah's father is the Marquess of Hatley, from what I remember."

"And Lord Welton is an Earl," Lady Amelia murmured, her gaze returned to the book again. "He, mayhap, has read of this supposed agreement and is now pursuing Lady Deborah. It would certainly improve his standing if he were to marry a Marquess' daughter."

"And yet, Lady Deborah has refused him."

"Mayhap making him deeply upset at her refusal?" Isobella considered, aloud. "But that does not mean that he would do anything against Lady Clara, surely? Nor could I understand why he might whisper about the Duke."

Isobella nodded slowly, her brow furrowing. "I cannot imagine why. His dislike of him was intense enough that he struck the Duke hard! I wonder if... " Thinking quickly, her heart began to thud wildly as an idea came to her. Her breath hitching, she took Lady Amelia's arm, holding it tightly. "What if Lord Welton saw the Duke as a threat?"

Lady Amelia's eyes flew wide. "A threat to his pursuit of Lady Deborah?"

"Yes, that is what I mean." Everything began to fall into place, leaving Isobella in a state of heightened anticipation as, finally, she saw a path ahead. "If Lord Welton believed that the Duke was pursuing Lady Deborah *or* that Lady Deborah herself was interested in the Duke himself, then might he not have acted in a way to push all thought of the Duke from Lady Deborah?"

"By spreading rumors about him," Lady Amelia said slowly, turning to look down at the book again. "He thinks that they have a connection, that they *ought* to marry because of this agreement. She rejects it, for it is much too old for her to take with any seriousness now, but Lord

Welton is determined. Pushing other gentlemen out of her path and out of her mind is his only course of action, and so, he begins to speak ill of the Duke."

Isobella swallowed hard. "More than that," she said, huskily, remembering the connection between Lord Welton and Lady Victoria. "He sets up a dark situation with Lady Clara and uses his cousin to have her believe that it was the Duke of Exeter." A shudder ran down her frame. "Mayhap *he* was the one who attacked Lady Clara."

"Goodness." Lady Amelia stared back at Isobella as each of them grappled with what they had only just begun to make sense of. "Then how do we prove it?"

"We must first speak to Lady Deborah," Isobella said, her eagerness to have the Duke proven innocent growing fiercely. "If she confirms what we think, then I must tell everything to the Duke. It will be up to him what he does with it all."

Lady Amelia nodded. "I will go and tell the others. When do you intend to speak to Lady Deborah?"

"This very afternoon, if I can," Isobella said, picking up the book and reading the few lines again. "We are so close to the truth, Amelia. I am *sure* of it."

"Forgive me for coming directly to the point – and for such a blunt question – but I must ask you something." Isobella, who had managed to find Lady Deborah without too much difficulty amongst the crowd of gentlemen and ladies at the fashionable hour, looked straight into the young lady's eyes. "Is Lord Welton pursuing you?"

"Lord Welton?" A flush began to creep up Lady Deborah's neck, rising into her cheeks. "I am sorry to hear that such a rumor has been making its way around London." She lifted her chin. "I am sorry to inform you that there is no connection whatsoever between myself and Lord Welton."

"Do not be sorry," Lady Amelia said, with a small smile. "Thank you for being so honest with us, Lady Deborah. We ask only because – "

"Because of what you witnessed, I am sure," Lady Deborah interrupted, looking at Isobella. "I was heartily ashamed of him for doing such a thing. There was no need for him to treat the Duke as he did. To hit him with such force was nothing short of disgraceful, and I am surprised the Duke did not call him out."

Isobella hesitated, wondering if she should press Lady Deborah further on that particular subject, choosing, in the end, to do so. "Lord Preston informed me that Lord Welton did so because he – the Duke, that is – had been maligning you and therefore, he felt bound to come to your defense."

Lady Deborah closed her eyes and shook her head. "That is not true in the least, I am afraid. You must also be aware that it is a lie, Lady Isobella." She opened her eyes as Isobella nodded. "I am sorry that you heard Lord Welton speak to the Duke as you did. I am not certain what to make of it all, for I cannot be sure that Lady Clara is telling the truth. I think she is speaking of what she believes to be the truth but that she cannot be entirely sure."

This was more than Isobella had been expecting and, seeing Lady Amelia's hopeful smile, pressed on. "Why is it that Lord Welton wishes to be so close to you, might I ask? He is seeking to pursue you, I think, but you are not inclined towards him."

"No, I am not." Lady Deborah sighed and looked away. "There is some old family agreement, evidently. Lord Welton discovered it quite recently and, since then, has been determined to marry me. My father has seen the agreement but says it does not carry any weight, for it was so long ago and without any legal binding that it need not affect us now."

"But Lord Welton persists."

When Lady Deborah returned her gaze to Isobella, tears were sparkling in her eyes. "He does. I have grown weary of it, and to see how he acted towards the Duke made me all the more disinclined towards him. I cannot tell why he chooses to pursue me so vehemently when there are many other young ladies, but I know he is near enough relentless!"

Sympathy rose in Isobella's heart. "That must be a weighty burden."

Lady Deborah's lips curved just a little. "It has been. For a time, I thought that the Duke of Exeter might be a gentleman worth considering, but after all that has happened, after all these rumors, I confess that I am now very uncertain."

"And what if that was all that Lord Welton intended?" Lady Amelia spoke gently, but Isobella could still see the shock that rippled into Lady Deborah's expression. "What if that was precisely what he wanted?"

The lady did not answer for some time, staring first at Lady Amelia and then looking to Isobella. Isobella herself said nothing, waiting for the lady to understand what they meant.

A shuddering exclamation broke from Lady Deborah's lips. She put her hands over her face, and both Isobella and Lady Amelia drew near at once, wanting both to comfort the lady and to hide her from society's prying eyes.

"I did not think for a moment that he would ever do such a thing," Lady Deborah whispered, her hands lowering as tears stained her cheeks. "Now that you have suggested it, however, I can see just how much truth there might be there! Of *course* he would want the Duke away from me, given just how much he wants me for himself."

Isobella looked at Lady Amelia, hope and sorrow twining together in her heart. "I am sorry to have made the suggestion, but I do think it is a possibility."

Lady Deborah sniffed, pulled her handkerchief from her pocket, and dabbed at her eyes. "You have been doing your best to defend the Duke, have you not?"

"I have." Isobella did not hold the truth back from the lady, choosing to be honest. "I believed him when he said he did not do any of those things to Lady Clara, that every rumor is false."

Another sniff came from Lady Deborah before she pushed her handkerchief away again. "I could not understand why Lady Clara believed it to be the Duke but Lady Victoria was so very convincing, I felt as though I had to accept it."

"Lady Victoria?"

Lady Deborah nodded. "We were both talking to the Duke and then, a strange noise came from a darker part of the gardens. I was not concerned by it, but Lady Victoria was terribly upset. She encouraged the Duke to go and see what the trouble was – and then, within a few moments, a loud cry came, and Lady Clara and Lady Sara rushed out towards the French doors. Lady Victoria grabbed my hand and tugged me after them, saying aloud that the Duke must have done something dreadful, but I am *sure* that the sound came from another part of the garden. She seemed quite determined to speak to Lady Clara and, indeed, caught her as she rushed into the ballroom." She sighed heavily. "I want to accept all that is said, but I fear I cannot. All the same, it feels wrong to doubt Lady Clara, given what happened to her."

This was all the confirmation Isobella needed. Lady Victoria had, for whatever reason, encouraged Lady Clara – and others, it seemed – to accept that the Duke of Exeter had been the one at fault. A deep breath filled her lungs as she closed her eyes, feeling as if a weight was lifting from her heart.

Quite what would happen now, she could not say, but the Duke, at least, would have all the information he needed to confront Lord Welton, if he so wished. What came after that, Isobella would not permit herself to think of. Not yet. Not until she knew for sure that all these lies and rumors were at an end.

Chapter Twenty

"So Lord Welton was the one who attacked Lady Clara?" Amos ran one hand over his eyes as the bluestockings all looked back at him. "Or can you not be sure of that?"

"We cannot be sure," Lady Rosalyn said. "But it is clear to us that Lord Welton and Lady Victoria are the ones who orchestrated all of this. Lord Welton was afraid that you were about to pursue Lady Deborah – or that she was hopeful that you might – and given that he felt he had a claim upon her already, he did what he had to to end that interest."

Amos let his gaze turn to Lady Isobella, who simply returned his look with a small smile. Yes, at one time, he had considered Lady Deborah, but that had only been a brief moment and had come *before* he'd realized just how much of a treasure Lady Isobella was. "This is... concerning."

"Yes, it is. However, we are sharing this all with you in the hope that you will know what to do next," Lady Isobella told him, her eyes never leaving his. "Lady Clara was in a great deal of confusion and upset about what had

179

happened, so it would not surprise me in the least if Lady Victoria, in rushing after her as we now know she did, made quite certain to emphasize that it had been you who had attacked her. I do not think there is anything that needs to be said to her."

"No, indeed not." Amos ran one hand over his chin, trying to think about what he would do and how he would confront Lord Welton. The bruise to his cheek had begun to fade, but the marks were still visible. Would that be enough for him to begin a conversation with the gentleman? It would have to be done in public somehow. "I should like to speak with Lord Welton, however. Mayhap the fashionable hour would be a place to speak with him?"

The bluestockings all glanced at each other, but Amos could not make out whether they agreed with his suggestion or not. After a few moments, Miss Trentworth spoke.

"You would certainly be guaranteed an audience, Your Grace. Although mayhap that is what you want?"

"I want the *ton* to hear what Lord Welton says, yes," Amos admitted. "How else am I to free my good name from the darkness that binds it at present?"

She nodded. "We understand entirely. Might I suggest, then, that we stand near to you? It might be that we are able to bring Lady Victoria into the conversation also."

Hope began to drive him. "I cannot tell you all how grateful I am to you for your assistance in all of this." Again, his gaze returned – and lingered – on Lady Isobella. "I do not know what I would have done had I been rejected." Even the thought made pain sting at his heart, though it faded quickly with the gentle smile that spread across her face. She had been his one thought when all of this had taken place, fearing that she would reject him. How grateful he was to her for her willingness to trust, to accept that he was not as cruel nor as dreadful as others believed! His path might have been a very different one otherwise.

"When are you to go?" Miss Sherwood asked, as Amos forced his gaze away from Lady Isobella. "The fashionable hour is not yet begun, if you were thinking of speaking with him this afternoon."

And once I have done so, I will be able to open my heart to Lady Isobella. It was that thought which drove him to his feet, to the determination to find Lord Welton just as soon as he could. "This afternoon, yes," he said, as the bluestockings all rose. "Might we meet in the park?"

Lady Amelia tilted her head. "Why do you not walk with Lady Isobella, and we will all follow at a distance?" she asked, as Lady Isobella ducked her head and blushed. "If we spy Lady Victoria, some of us will be able to go and speak with her also."

"A capital idea." He looked back at Lady Isobella. "If you would be willing, of course?"

Her head lifted, her eyes sparkling whilst pink flushed her cheeks. "I would be, Your Grace."

"Then I shall see you – see you *all* – very soon," he said, making his way from them all, knowing he now had to return home to prepare for the fashionable hour. "Thank you all, from the very depths of my heart."

Walking arm in arm with Lady Isobella, Amos felt his heart squeeze with the vast affection and admiration he felt for her. It was easy enough to ignore the glances that certain members of the *ton* sent them, for he did not care for anything other than Lady Isobella and her presence beside him.

"You have done so much for me, Lady Isobella," he

murmured, as they walked. "I do not think I will ever be able to express my gratitude."

She looked up at him, her copper curls brushing her temples. "There is no need, Your Grace. I am only glad that it is all soon to come to an end and your good name restored."

"I only really needed your acceptance of me," he said, revealing just a little of his heart to her. "If you had trusted me, then my heart would have been satisfied."

The smile on her face grew, but she dipped her head, letting her gaze pull from his. A trifle frustrated with himself, Amos opened his mouth to say more, only for someone to catch his elbow.

"You have walked directly past him, Your Grace." Lady Amelia's eyes twinkled. "There, on your left. Lady Rosalyn and Miss Trentworth have already seen Lady Victoria and have gone to speak with her. Lady Deborah is also present, and they may bring her to join you."

A little embarrassed, Amos thanked her and then turned his head, seeing Lord Welton laughing at something another fellow had said. With a look at Lady Isobella, he took in a deep breath and then, setting his shoulders, strode towards the gentleman. Now was the time for confidence, for determination. He had to find a way to make Lord Welton admit what he had done.

"Welton." His voice was commanding as he approached, dropping Lady Isobella's hand from his arm so she could stay a little back from him. "You have been spreading yet more rumors about me, I see."

Lord Welton's smile grew dark as Amos drew near, the other gentlemen with him stepping back at once. "Your Grace," he said, his lip curling. "I have said nothing but the truth, I assure you."

"Except I did not *ever* insult Lady Deborah," Amos answered, loudly enough for more than a few present to hear. "She herself has said such a thing."

Lord Welton snorted. "A likely story. You say such a thing only to cover your guilt."

"There were many present in the library who overheard our conversation," Amos replied, firmly, refusing to show a single iota of uncertainty or discomfort. This, even though his heart was beating wildly, worry nipping at his mind. What if Lord Welton did not admit to anything?

"They will all have been manipulated by you," Lord Welton responded. "I know what I heard, and *I*, at least, am a gentleman. I acted just as a gentleman ought when a lady is insulted."

"Except I was not insulted by the Duke."

Amos's head turned, just as Lady Deborah, Lady Victoria, and the other bluestockings came to join them. Lady Victoria, Amos noticed, moved to stand a little closer to her cousin, her expression pinched.

"I was upset by you and your determination to have my agreement to marry you," Lady Deborah continued, her eyes glistening with a hint of tears. "The Duke said not a word about me. I am utterly ashamed of you, Welton. How could you have struck the Duke so without cause?"

This brought a hesitancy to Lord Welton's expression, his mouth opening and then closing again, the cruel smile now gone completely. "I – I am sure I heard him – "

"You did not." Lady Isobella spoke now, coming to stand beside Lady Deborah. "I was there also, and he did not say a word against her."

Lady Victoria let out a loud sigh, drawing everyone's attention. "Why must you be so disagreeable towards my cousin? He was only doing his best to protect Lady Deborah."

"By spreading malicious rumors about me?" Amos countered as the color began to drain from Lady Victoria's face. "By pretending that I had attacked Lady Clara in the gardens when, in fact, *he* had been the one to do it, with the sole intention of making sure that my name was sunk into the mud?"

It felt as if the entirety of Hyde Park fell silent as Amos spoke, but he fixed his gaze on Lady Victoria, wondering if, given her pallor, she might be the one who would admit the truth before Lord Welton did.

"And he convinced you to help him, did he not?" Lady Isobella spoke quietly, but her words sounded like thunderclaps. "It was all in aid of him gaining Lady Deborah's acceptance of his hand, was it not?"

"Preposterous!" Lord Welton threw up his hands, anger sparking in his eyes. "All of this is nonsense."

Lady Deborah took a step closer to Lady Victoria. "We are friends, are we not?" she asked, her voice thin with tears. "You would not have done something so terrible, would you?" When Lady Victoria said nothing, Lady Deborah closed her eyes, a tear falling to her cheek. "You were so determined to have the Duke rush into the gardens, to hear what that sound was. Thereafter, you nearly dragged me into the ballroom, rushing over to Lady Clara and leaving me behind. What was it you said to her?"

"We can ask her easily enough," Miss Trentworth said, her eyes narrowing as she looked to Lord Welton. "I am quite certain she would say that Lady Victoria convinced her that it *was* the Duke of Exeter who had frightened her so."

Amos clasped his hands behind his back. "Your deter-

mination to have Lady Deborah is verging on cruel manip-
ulation, Welton," he said, as Lady Deborah let out a sob.
"Why would you do such a dreadful thing? She has
already refused you, has told you that she does not want to
accept you, and still, you pursue her? You chase her so
relentlessly that she is near broken by your attempts to
convince her!"

"Oh, Deborah." Lady Victoria's eyes welled with tears
as she reached out for her friend, as Lord Welton's face
turned a shade of deep red. "I did not know you had refused
him. He told me that you were considering him, begged me
to help him convince you, and pull you from the Duke. He
told me about the state of his affairs, about your connection
would restore all and – "

"Enough, Victoria!" Lord Welton rounded on her,
coming closer to her with his hand raised as if to strike her.
Amos acted in an instant, grabbing the man's arm and
yanking him backwards, before pushing his arm up his back.
Lord Welton cried out in pain whilst Lady Victoria covered
her mouth with her hand, blinking back tears.

"Then it is true," one of the gentlemen watching said,
loudly enough for Amos to hear. "Lord *Welton* was the one
responsible for attacking Lady Clara."

"I had to drive you away!" Lord Welton spat, his face
contorted with both anger and pain as Amos finally released
him, pushing him back so there was distance between them.
"Lady Deborah is *mine*. I need her. I must have her, else my
estate is ruined!"

Lady Deborah let out a sob. "Then it is all about my
fortune?"

"When I found that agreement, it was the answer to my
prayers," Lord Welton hissed, as everyone around him took
a step back, wanting now to distance themselves from him.

185

"You *must* do your duty, Deborah! You must marry me and
– "

"She will *never* marry you." A voice that Amos had
never heard before broke in, a gentleman with a greying
beard and sharp, brown eyes coming to stand beside Lady
Deborah, a comforting arm around her shoulders. "How
could you do such a thing, Welton? How *dare* you treat not
only my daughter but Lady Clara *and* the Duke of Exeter
with such disrespect and disregard? They are not playthings
for you to do with just as you please, so you might gain your
own ends! I tell you this now, she will *never* marry you. And
given what has just been revealed, I think it is highly
unlikely that you shall ever marry well at all."

Relief swept through Amos, as if he had stepped out of
the cold into the blazing sunshine. Looking around for Lady
Isobella, he found his gaze centering on her, the ache in his
heart forcing him towards her. There was no need for him
to linger any more, no need for him to stay by Lord Welton
and say anything further. The truth had been revealed, and
now, slowly but surely, the *ton* would hear of it. His reputation was restored, his name no longer maligned, and Lady
Isobella was the cause of it all.

"Lady Isobella." Catching her hand in his, he bowed
over it. "How ever am I to thank you?"

When he lifted his head, she was smiling at him. "Your
happiness and relief are all that I need, Your Grace."

Amos did not release her hand. "I know that now may
not be the best time to speak of certain... matters, Lady
Isobella, but I cannot help myself." Swallowing thickly, he
looked down at their joined hands. "I went to speak to your
brother recently."

"You did?" The surprise in her voice made him lift his
head. "For what reason?"

"Because I cannot stop thinking about you, Lady Isobella. My every moment is caught up with you," he confessed, as she began to blink rapidly. "I wanted to make certain that I would have his consent should I seek to court you. However, whilst it was given, it was emphasized that the decision had to be yours and yours alone."

Lady Isobella pressed her lips together and looked away. "I – I am not sure as to what I ought to say."

Amos did not say anything further, wondering if he should say anything about what he had learned from her brother, but choosing not to do so. If she wished to express it, then that would be her decision.

"I am afraid." Even in the hubbub of activity behind them, her voice was clear as if she were the only one speaking. "I want to trust you, Your Grace. I want to offer you my heart, but I am afraid."

He nodded slowly. "Is there anything that I can say to make you trust me?"

Her eyes closed, and she pressed her lips flat for a few moments. "I have trusted in the past, Your Grace."

"Exeter, please."

That made her cheeks darken. "Exeter. I have trusted in the past and have had not one but three gentlemen break that trust. The latter broke my heart, and I swore I would never let myself trust again."

"And now?" He waited, seeing her shoulders drop as she considered his words. "Even now, will you hold to that promise?"

Epilogue

Isobella did not know what to say. Her heart was roaring with both hope, anticipation, and fear, and yet, as much as she wanted to draw near to the Duke, the more her worries pulled her back.

"I swore I would be a spinster," she said, eventually, the Duke's thumb running backwards and forward over her hand. "I told myself that I have already endured too much pain and heartbreak to ever let myself have such hope again."

The Duke leaned down just a little. "Do you mean to say, Isobella, that you have that hope all the same?"

Closing her eyes so that she could not see the fervency in his gaze, she nodded, her fears waging war against the swell of anticipation. "I have begun to feel things I never wanted to feel again," she admitted, forcing the words out. "I have told myself that I am nothing but a fool, and still, such feelings endure."

"I do not think you a fool."

Her eyes opened.

"I think you the most wonderful young lady," he swore,

the fervency burning in his eyes beginning to swallow up her fears. "You have such an honest, kind heart, a goodness within you that has reached into my very soul and taken hold of me. When these rumors first came to my ears, it was only you I thought of. I was so very afraid that you would believe them and that you would turn from me." He smiled, and Isobella's heart lurched. "When you did not, the relief and the joy I felt were overpowering. Now, I confess to you that I think I am quite in love with you, Isobella. I want very much to court you – nay, to marry you, if you would have me! However, in understanding what you have suffered, if you choose to step back from this, then I swear I shall do nothing more. I will not pursue you, I will not beg you, I will not demand that you reconsider. Instead, I shall accept your decision and respect the distance you put between us."

Tears pricked at the corners of her eyes. Strangely enough, in saying such a thing to her, the Duke had revealed the truth of his heart to her. He cared about her enough to state that, even if she refused him, even if it would cause him pain, he would respect what she determined. Did that not speak of a genuine affection? Could she not let herself trust this one last time?

"I – I do not want distance." A single tear fell to her cheek, and she dashed it away quickly. "The thought of being apart from you is injurious to me."

"Then will you accept my courtship?" he asked, the hope in his voice sending sparks of light into his eyes. "If not, the offer of my hand? I am a Duke, after all, and I could fetch a Special License so we could marry tomorrow, if we wished!" Bending his head, he brought her hand to his lips and kissed the back of it. "I want you to be able to trust in my love, Isobella. I swear to you, I will do anything you want, anything you need to prove to you that I will never

189

step away from you. I am not like those other fellows, I swear it."

Isobella considered him, her heart pulling free of the shadows of the past that bound it so tightly. The Duke was not like as Lord Brookmire, Lord Pollock, and Lord Hogarth had been, she could see that. She *knew* that, for in the time they had spent together, had he not always been honest and open with her? This was what her heart had been trying to tell her for so long. She could see that now, could see just how much she had tried to ignore it, had tried to hide it and dismiss it.

But no longer.

Her heart leapt up, the pain swallowed up by the profession of his love. With a soft smile and tears in her eyes, she stepped closer to him. "Yes."

"Yes?" The Duke's eyebrows shot upwards, a broad smile spreading across his face. "Yes to courtship? To marriage? To the Special License?"

She laughed and, despite the crowd, put her arms around his neck and let him hold her tightly. What did it matter? They were to be married soon. "Yes to it all," she whispered in his ear, a joy like nothing she had ever felt before flooding her. "Yes to courtship, yes to marriage, yes to the Special License if you wish it!" Leaning back, she looked into his eyes and smiled. "And yes, most of all, to love."

My Dear Reader

Thank you for reading and supporting my books! I hope this story brought you some escape from the real world into the always captivating Regency world. A good story, especially one with a happy ending, just brightens your day and makes you feel good! If you enjoyed the book, would you leave a review on Amazon? Reviews are always appreciated.

Below is a complete list of all my books! Why not click and see if one of them can keep you entertained for a few hours?

The Duke's Daughters Series
The Duke's Daughters: A Sweet Regency Romance Boxset
A Rogue for a Lady
My Restless Earl
Rescued by an Earl
In the Arms of an Earl
The Reluctant Marquess (Prequel)

A Smithfield Market Regency Romance
The Smithfield Market Romances: A Sweet Regency Romance Boxset
The Rogue's Flower
Saved by the Scoundrel
Mending the Duke
The Baron's Malady

The Returned Lords of Grosvenor Square
The Returned Lords of Grosvenor Square: A Regency
Romance Boxset
The Waiting Bride
The Long Return
The Duke's Saving Grace
A New Home for the Duke

The Spinsters Guild
The Spinsters Guild: A Sweet Regency Romance Boxset
A New Beginning
The Disgraced Bride
A Gentleman's Revenge
A Foolish Wager
A Lord Undone

Convenient Arrangements
Convenient Arrangements: A Regency Romance
Collection
A Broken Betrothal
In Search of Love
Wed in Disgrace
Betrayal and Lies
A Past to Forget
Engaged to a Friend

Landon House
Landon House: A Regency Romance Boxset
Mistaken for a Rake
A Selfish Heart
A Love Unbroken
A Christmas Match
A Most Suitable Bride

An Expectation of Love

Second Chance Regency Romance
Second Chance Regency Romance Boxset
Loving the Scarred Soldier
Second Chance for Love
A Family of her Own
A Spinster No More

Soldiers and Sweethearts
Soldiers and Sweethearts Boxset
To Trust a Viscount
Whispers of the Heart
Dare to Love a Marquess
Healing the Earl
A Lady's Brave Heart

Ladies on their Own: Governesses and Companions
Ladies on their Own Boxset
More Than a Companion
The Hidden Governess
The Companion and the Earl
More than a Governess
Protected by the Companion

Lost Fortunes, Found Love
Lost Fortunes, Found Love Boxset
A Viscount's Stolen Fortune
For Richer, For Poorer
Her Heart's Choice
A Dreadful Secret
Their Forgotten Love
His Convenient Match

Only for Love

Only for Love : A Clean Regency Boxset

The Heart of a Gentleman

A Lord or a Liar

The Earl's Unspoken Love

The Viscount's Unlikely Ally

The Highwayman's Hidden Heart

Miss Millington's Unexpected Suitor

Waltzing with Wallflowers

Waltzing with Wallflowers: A Regency Romance Boxset

The Wallflower's Unseen Charm

The Wallflower's Midnight Waltz

Wallflower Whispers

The Ungainly Wallflower

The Determined Wallflower

The Wallflower's Secret (Revenge of the Wallflowers series)

The Wallflower's Choice

Whispers of the Ton

The Truth about the Earl

The Truth about the Rogue

The Truth about the Marquess

The Truth about the Viscount

The Truth about the Duke

The Truth about the Lady

Bluestocking Book Club

The Earl's Error

The Marquess' Painting

The Missing Book

The Viscount's Forgery

The Duke's Scandal

Christmas in London Series
The Uncatchable Earl
The Undesirable Duke

Christmas Kisses Series
Christmas Kisses Box Set
The Lady's Christmas Kiss
The Viscount's Christmas Queen
Her Christmas Duke

Christmas Stories
Love and Christmas Wishes: Three Regency Romance
Novellas
A Family for Christmas
Mistletoe Magic: A Regency Romance
Heart, Homes & Holidays: A Sweet Romance Anthology

Happy Reading!
All my love,
Rose

A Sneak Peek of The
Heart of a Gentleman

Chapter One

"Thank you again for sponsoring me through this Season." Lady Cassandra Chilton pressed her hands together tightly, a delighted smile spreading across her features as excitement quickened her heart. Having spent a few years in London, with the rest of her family, it was now finally her turn to come out into society. "I would not have been able to come to London had you not been so generous."

Norah, Lady Yardley smiled softly and slipped her arm through Cassandra's.

"I am just as glad as you to have you here, cousin." A small sigh slipped from her, and her expression was gentle. "It does not seem so long ago that I was here myself, to make my Come Out."

Cassandra's happiness faded just a little

"Your first marriage was not of great length, I recall." Pressing her lips together immediately, she winced, dropping her head, hugely embarrassed by her own forthrightness "Forgive me. I ought not to be speaking of such things."

Thankfully, Lady Yardley chuckled.

"You need not be so concerned, my dear. You are right to say that my first marriage was not of long duration, but I *have* found a great happiness since then - more than that, in fact. I have found a love which has brought me such wondrous contentment that I do not think I should ever have been able to live without it." At this, Cassandra found herself sighing softly, her eyes roving around the London streets as though they might land on the very gentleman who would thereafter bring her the same love, within her own heart, that her cousin spoke of. "But you must be cautious," her cousin continued. "There are many gentlemen in London – even more during the Season – and not *all* of them will seek the same sort of love match as you. Therefore, you must always be cautious, my dear."

A little surprised at this, Cassandra looked at her cousin as they walked along the London streets.

"I must be cautious?"

Her cousin nodded sagely.

"Yes, most careful, my dear. Society is not always as it appears. It can be a fickle friend." Lady Yardley glanced at Cassandra then quickly smiled - a smile which Cassandra did not immediately believe. "Pray, do not allow me to concern you, not when you have only just arrived in London!" She shook her head and let out an exasperated sigh, evidently directed towards herself. "No doubt you will have a wonderful Season. With so much to see and to enjoy, I am certain that these months will be delightful."

Cassandra allowed herself a small smile, her shoulders relaxing in gentle relief. She had always assumed that London society would be warm and welcoming and, whilst there was always the danger of scandal, that danger came only from young ladies or gentlemen choosing to behave improperly. Given that she was quite determined *not* to behave so, there could be no danger of scandal for her!

"I assure you, Norah, that I shall be impeccable in my behavior and in my speech. You need not concern yourself over that."

Lady Yardley touched her hand for a moment.

"I am sure that you shall. I have never once considered otherwise." She offered a quick smile. "But you will also learn a great deal about society and the gentlemen within it – and that will stand you in good stead."

Still not entirely certain, and pondering what her cousin meant, Cassandra found her thoughts turned in an entirely new direction when she saw someone she recognized. Miss Bridget Wynch was accompanied by another young lady who Cassandra knew, and with a slight squeal of excitement, she made to rush towards them – somehow managing to drag Lady Yardley with her. When Cassandra turned to apologize, her cousin laughingly disentangled herself and then urged Cassandra to continue to her friends. Cassandra did so without hesitation and, despite the fact it was in the middle of London, the three young ladies embraced each other openly, their voices high with excitement. Over the last few years, they had come to know each other as they had accompanied various elder siblings to London, alongside their parents. Now it was to be their turn and the joy of that made Cassandra's heart sing.

"You are here then, Cassandra." Lady Almeria grasped her hand tightly. "And you were so concerned that your father would not permit you to come."

"It was not that he was unwilling to permit me to attend, rather that he was concerned that he would be on the continent at the time," Cassandra explained. "In that regard, he was correct, for both my father *and* my mother have taken leave of England, and have gone to my father's properties on the continent. I am here, however, and stay now with my cousin." Turning, she gestured to Lady Yardley who was standing only a short distance away, a warm smile on her face. She did not move forward, as though she was unwilling to interrupt the conversation and, with a smile of gratitude, Cassandra turned back to her friends. "We are to make our first appearances in Society tomorrow." Stating this, she let out a slow breath. "How do you each feel?"

With a slight squeal, Miss Wynch closed her eyes and shuddered.

"Yes, we are, and I confess that I am quite terrified." Taking a breath, she pressed one hand to her heart. "I am very afraid that I will make a fool of myself in some way."

"As am I," Lady Almeria agreed. "I am afraid that I shall trip over my gown and fall face first in front of the most important people of the *ton*! Then what shall be said of me?"

"They will say that you may not be the most elegant young lady to dance with?" Cassandra suggested, as her friends giggled. "However, I am quite sure that you will have a great deal of poise – as you always do – and will be able to control your nerves quite easily. You will not so much as stumble."

"I thank you for your faith in me."

Lady Almeria let out a slow breath.

"Our other friends will be present also," Miss Wynch added. "How good it will be to see them again – both at our presentation and at the ball in the evening!"

Cassandra smiled at the thought of the ball, her stomach twisting gently with a touch of nervousness.

"I admit to being excited about our first ball also. I do

wonder which gentlemen we shall dance with." Lady Almeria swiveled her head around, looking at the many passersby before leaning forward a little more and dropping her voice low. "I am hopeful that one or two may become of significant interest to us."

Cassandra's smile fell.

"My cousin has warned me to be cautious when it comes to the gentlemen of London." Still a little disconcerted by what Lady Yardley had said to her, Cassandra gave her friends a small shrug. "I do not understand precisely what she meant, but there is something about the gentlemen of London of which we must be careful. My cousin has not explained to me precisely what that is as yet, but states that there is much I must learn. I confess to you, since we have all been in London before, for previous Seasons – albeit not for ourselves – I did not think that there would be a great deal for me to understand."

"I do not know what things Lady Yardley speaks of," Miss Wynch agreed, a small frown between her eyebrows now. "My elder sister did not have any difficulty with *her* husband. When they met, they were so delighted with each other they were wed within six weeks."

"I confess I know very little about Catherine's engagement and marriage," Lady Almeria replied, speaking of her elder sister who was some ten years her senior. "But I *do* know that Amanda had a little trouble, although I believe that came from the realization that she had to choose which gentleman was to be her suitor. She had *three* gentlemen eager to court her – all deserving gentlemen too – and therefore, she had some trouble in deciding who was best suited."

Cassandra frowned, her nose wrinkling.

"I could not say anything about my brother's marriage, but my sister did wait until her second Season before she accepted a gentleman's offer of courtship. She spoke very little to me of any difficulties, however - and therefore, I do not understand what my cousin means." A small sigh escaped her. "I do wish that my sister and I had been a little closer. She might have spoken to me of whatever difficulties she faced, whether they were large or small, but in truth, she said very little to me. Had she done so, then I might be already aware of whatever it is that Lady Yardley wishes to convey."

Miss Wynch put one hand on her arm.

"I am sure that we shall find out soon enough." She shrugged. "I do not think that you need to worry about it either, given that we have more than enough to think about! Maybe after our come out, Lady Yardley will tell you all."

Cassandra took a deep breath and let herself smile as the tension flooded out of her.

"Yes, you are right." Throwing a quick glance back towards her cousin, who was still standing nearby, she spread both hands. "Regardless of what is said, I am still determined to marry for love."

"As am I." Lady Almeria's lips tipped into a soft smile. "In fact, I think that all of us – our absent friends included – are determined to marry for love. Did we not all say so last Season, as we watched our sisters and brothers make their matches? I find myself just as resolved today as I was then. I do not think our desires a foolish endeavor."

Cassandra shook her head.

"Nor do I, although my brother would have a different opinion, given that he trumpeted how excellent a match he made with his new bride."

With a wry laugh, she tilted her head, and looked from one friend to the other.

"And my sister would have laughed at us for such a

suggestion, I confess," Lady Almeria agreed. "She states practicality to be the very best of situations, but I confess I dream of more."

"As do I." A slightly wistful expression came over Miss Wynch as she clasped both hands to her heart, her eyes closing for a moment. "I wish to know that a gentleman's heart is filled only with myself, rather than looking at me as though I am some acquisition suitable for his household."

Such a description made Cassandra shudder as she nodded fervently. To be chosen by a gentleman simply due to her father's title, or for her dowry, would be most displeasing. To Cassandra's mind, it would not bring any great happiness.

"Then I have a proposal." Cassandra held out her hands, one to each of her friends. "What say you we promise each other – here and now, that we shall *only* marry for love and shall support each other in our promises to do so? We can speak to our other friends and seek their agreement also."

Catching her breath, Lady Almeria nodded fervently, her smile spreading across her face.

"It sounds like a wonderful idea."

"I quite agree." Miss Wynch smiled back at her, reaching to grasp Cassandra's hand. "We shall speak to the others soon, I presume?"

"Yes, of course. We shall have a merry little band together and, in time, we are certain to have success." Cassandra sighed contentedly, the last flurries of tension going from her. "We will all find ourselves suitable matches with gentlemen to whom we can lose our hearts, knowing that their hearts love us in return."

As her friends smiled, Cassandra's heart began to soar. This Season was going to be an excellent one, she was sure.

Yes, she had her cousin's warnings, but she also had her friends' support in her quest to find a gentleman who would love her; a gentleman she would carry in her heart for all of her days. Surely such a fellow would not be so difficult to find?

Chapter Two

"I should like to hear something... significant... about you this Season."

Jonathan rolled his eyes, knowing precisely what his mother expected. This was now his fourth Season in London and, as yet, he had not found himself a bride – much to his mother's chagrin, of course. On his part, it was quite deliberate and, although he had stated as much to his mother on various occasions, it did not seem to alter her attempts to encourage him toward matrimony.

"You are aware that you did not have to come to London with me, Mother?" Jonathan shrugged his shoulders. "If you had remained at home, then you would not have suffered as much concern, surely?"

"It is a legitimate concern, which I would suffer equally, no matter where I am!" his mother shot back fiercely. "You have not given me any expectation of a forthcoming marriage and I continually wonder and worry over the lack of an heir! You are the Marquess of Sherbourne! You have responsibilities!"

Jonathan scowled.

"Responsibilities I take seriously, Mother. However, I will not be forced into–"

"I have already heard whispers of your various entanglements during last Season. I can hardly imagine that this Season will be any better."

At this, Jonathan took a moment to gather himself, trying to control the fierce surge of anger now burning in his soul. When he spoke, it was with a quietness he could barely keep hold of.

"I assure you, such whispers have been greatly exaggerated. I am not a scoundrel."

He could tell immediately that this did not please his mother, for she shook her head and let out a harsh laugh.

"I do not believe that," she stated, her tone still fierce. "Especially when my *dear* friend, Lady Edmonds, tells me that you were attempting to entice her daughter into your arms!" Her eyes closed tight. "The fact that she is still willing to even be my friend is very generous indeed."

A slight pang of guilt edged into Jonathan's heart, but he ignored it with an easy shrug of his shoulders.

"Do you truly think that Lady Hannah was so unwilling? That I had to coerce her somehow?" Seeing how his mother pressed one hand to her mouth, he rolled his eyes for the second time. "It is the truth I tell you, Mother. Whether you wish to believe me or not, any rumors you have heard have been greatly exaggerated. For example, Lady Hannah was the one who came to seek *me* out, rather than it being me pursuing her."

His mother rose from her chair, her chin lifting and her face a little flushed.

"I will not believe that Lady Hannah, who is so delicate a creature, would even have *dreamt* of doing such a thing as that!"

"You very may very well not believe it, and that would not surprise me, given that everyone else holds much the same opinion." Spreading both hands, Jonathan let out a small sigh. "I may not be eager to wed, Mother, but I certainly am not a scoundrel or a rogue, as you appear to believe me to be."

His mother looked away, her hands planted on her hips, and Jonathan scowled, frustrated by his mother's lack of belief in his character. During last Season, he had been utterly astonished when Lady Hannah had come to speak with him directly, only to attempt to draw him into some sort of assignation. And she only in her first year out in Society as well! Jonathan had always kept far from those young ladies who were newly out – even, as in this case, from those who had been so very obvious in their eagerness. No doubt being a little upset by his lack of willingness, Lady Hannah had gone on to tell her mother a deliberate untruth about him, suggesting that *he* had been the one to try to negotiate something warm between them. And now, it seemed, his own mother believed that same thing. It was not the first time that such rumors had been spread about gentlemen – himself included and, on some occasions, Jonathan admitted, the rumors had come about because of his actions. But other whispers, such as this, were grossly unfair. Yet who would believe the word of a supposedly roguish gentleman over that of a young lady? There was, Jonathan considered, very little point in arguing.

"I will not go near Lady Hannah this Season, if that is what is concerning you." With a slight lift of his shoulders, Jonathan tried to smile at his mother, but only received an angry glare in return. "I assure you that I have no interest in Lady Hannah! She is not someone I would consider even stepping out with, were I given the opportunity." Protesting his innocence was futile, he knew, but yet the words kept coming. "I do not even think her overly handsome."

"Are you stating that she is ugly?"

Jonathan closed his eyes, stifling a groan. It seemed that he could say nothing which would bring his mother any satisfaction. The only thing to please her would be if he declared himself betrothed to a suitable young lady. At present, however, he had very little intention of doing anything of the sort. He was quite content with his life, such as it was. The time to continue the family line would come soon enough, but he could give it a few more years until he had to consider it.

"No, mother, Lady Hannah is not ugly." Seeing how her frown lifted just a little, he took his opportunity to escape. "Now, if you would excuse me, I have an afternoon tea to attend." His mother's eyebrows lifted with evident hope, but Jonathan immediately set her straight. "With Lord and Lady Yardley," he added, aware of how quickly her features slumped again. "I have no doubt that you will be a little frustrated by the fact that my ongoing friendship with Lord and Lady Yardley appears to be the most significant connection in my life, but he is a dear friend and his wife has become so also. Surely you can find no complaint there!" His mother sniffed and looked away, and Jonathan, believing now that there was very little he could say to even bring a smile to his mother's face, turned his steps towards the door. "Good afternoon, Mother."

So saying, he strode from the room, fully aware of the heavy weight of expectation that his mother continually placed upon his shoulders. He could not give her what she wanted, and her ongoing criticism was difficult to hear. She did not have proof of his connection to Lady Hannah but, all the same, thought poorly of him. She would criticize his close acquaintance with Lord and Lady Yardley also! His friendships were quickly thrown aside, as were his explanations and his pleadings of innocence - there was nothing he could say or do that would bring her even a hint of satisfaction, and Jonathan had no doubt that, during this Season, he would be a disappointment to her all over again.

* * *

"Good afternoon, Yardley."

His friend beamed at him, turning his head for a moment as he poured two measures of brandy into two separate glasses.

"Sherbourne! Good afternoon, do come in. It appears to be an excellent afternoon, does it not?"

Jonathan did so, his eyes on his friend, gesturing to the brandy on the table.

"It will more than excellent once you hand me the glass which I hope is mine."

Lord Yardley chuckled and obliged him.

"And yet, it seems as though you are troubled all the same," he remarked, as Jonathan took a sip of what he knew to be an excellent French brandy. "Come then, what troubles you this time?" Lifting an eyebrow, he grinned as Jonathan groaned aloud. "I am certain it will have something to do with your dear mother."

Letting out an exasperated breath, Jonathan gesticulated in the air as Lord Yardley took a seat opposite him.

"She wishes me to be just as you are." Jonathan took a small sip of his brandy. "Whereas I am less and less inclined to wed myself to *any* young lady who has her approval... simply because she will have my mother's approval!"

Lord Yardley chuckled and then took a sip from his glass.

"That is difficult indeed! You are quite right to state that *you* will be the one to decide when you wed... so long as it is not simply because you are avoiding your responsibilities."

"I am keenly aware of my responsibilities, which is precisely *why* I avoid matrimony. I already have a great deal of demands on my time – I can only imagine that to add a wife to that burden would only increase it!"

"You are quite mistaken."

Jonathan chuckled darkly.

"You only say so because your wife is an exceptional lady. I think you one of the *few* gentlemen who finds themselves so blessed."

Lord Yardley shrugged.

"Then I must wonder if you believe the state of matrimony to be a death knell to a gentleman's heart. I can assure you it is quite the opposite."

"You say that only because you have found contentment," Jonathan shot back quickly. "There are many gentlemen who do not find themselves so comfortable."

Lord Yardley shrugged.

"There may be more than you know." He picked up his brandy glass again. "And if that is what you seek from your forthcoming marriage to whichever young lady you choose, then why do you not simply search for a suitable match, rather than doing very little other than entertain yourself throughout the Season? You could find a lady who would bring you a great deal of contentment, I am sure."

Resisting the urge to roll his eyes, Jonathan spread both hands, one still clutching his brandy, the other one empty.

"Because I do not feel the same urgency about the matter as my mother," he stated firmly. "When the time is right, I will find an excellent young lady who will fill my heart with such great affection that I will be unable to do anything but look into her eyes and find myself lost. *Then* I will know that she is the one I ought to wed. However, until that moment comes, I will continue on, just as I am at present." For a moment he thought that his friend would laugh at him, but much to his surprise, Lord Yardley simply nodded in agreement. There was not even a hint of a smile on his lips, but rather a gentle understanding in his eyes which spoke of acceptance of all that Jonathan had said. "Let us talk of something other than my present situation." Throwing back the rest of his brandy, and with a great and contented sigh, Jonathan set the glass back down on the table to his right. "Your other guests have not arrived as yet, I see. Are you hoping for a jovial afternoon?"

"A cheerful afternoon, certainly, although we will not be overwhelmed by too many guests today." Lord Yardley grinned. "It is a little unfortunate that I shall soon have to return to my estate." His smile faded a little. "I do not like the idea of being away from my wife, but there are many improvements taking place at the estate which must be overseen." His lips pulled to one side for a moment. "Besides which, my wife has her cousin to chaperone this Season."

"Her cousin?" Repeating this, Jonathan frowned as his friend nodded. "You did not mention this to me before."

"Did I not?" Lord Yardley replied mildly, waving one hand as though it did not matter. "Yes, my wife is to be chaperoning her cousin for the duration of the Season. The girl's parents are both on the continent, you understand, and given that she would not have much of a coming out otherwise, my wife thought it best to offer."

Jonathan tried to ignore the frustration within him at

the fact that his friend would not be present for the Season, choosing instead to nod.

"How very kind of her. And what is the name of this cousin?"

"Lady Cassandra Chilton." Lord Yardley's gaze flew towards the door. "No doubt you will meet her this afternoon. I do not know what is taking them so long but, then again, I have never been a young lady about to make her first appearance in Society."

Jonathan blinked. Clearly this was more than just an afternoon tea. This Lady Cassandra would be present this afternoon so that she might become acquainted with a few of those within society. Why Lord Yardley had not told him about this before, Jonathan did not know – although it was very like his friend to forget about such details.

"Lady Cassandra is being presented this afternoon?"

His friend nodded.

"Yes, as we speak. I did offer to go with them, of course, but was informed she was already nervous enough, and would be quite contented with just my dear wife standing beside her."

Jonathan nodded and was about to make some remark about how difficult a moment it must be for a young lady to be presented to the Queen, only for the door to open and Lady Yardley herself to step inside.

"Ah, Lord Sherbourne. How delighted I am to see you."

With a genuine smile on her face, she waved at him to remain seated rather than attempt to get up to greet her.

"Good afternoon, Lady Yardley. I do hope the presentation went well?"

"Exceptionally well. Cassandra has just gone up to change out of her presentation gown – those gowns which the Queen requires are so outdated and uncomfortable! She will join us shortly."

The lady threw a broad smile in the direction of her husband, who then rose immediately from his chair to go towards her. Taking her hands, he pressed a kiss to the back of one and then to the back of the other. It was a display of affection usually reserved only for private moments, but Jonathan was well used to such things between Lord and Lady Yardley. In many ways, he found it rather endearing.

"I am sure that Cassandra did very well with you beside her."

Lady Yardley smiled at her husband.

"She has a great deal of strength," she replied, quietly. "I find her quite remarkable. Indeed, I was proud to be there beside her."

"I have only just been hearing about your cousin, Lady Yardley. I do hope to be introduced to her very soon." Shifting in his chair, Jonathan waved his empty glass at Lord Yardley, who laughed but went in search of the brandy regardless. "You are sponsoring her through the Season, I understand."

His gaze now fixed itself on Lady Yardley, aware of that soft smile on her face.

"Yes, I am." Settling herself in her chair, she let out a small sigh as she did so. "I have no doubt that she will be a delight to society. She is young and beautiful and very well-considered, albeit a little naïve."

A slight frown caught Jonathan's forehead.

"Naïve?"

Lady Yardley nodded.

"Yes, just as every young lady new to society has been, and will be for years to come. She is quite certain that she will find herself hopelessly in love with the very best of a gentleman and that he will seek to marry her by the end of the Season."

"Such things do happen, my dear."

Lady Yardley laughed softly at Lord Yardley's remark, reaching across from her chair to grasp her husband's hand.

"I am not saying that they do not, only that my dear cousin thinks that all will be marvelously well for her in society and that the *ton* is a welcoming creature rather than one to be most cautious of. I, however, am much more on my guard. Not every gentleman who seeks her out will be looking to marry her. Not every gentleman who seeks her out will believe in the concept of love."

"Love?" Jonathan snorted, rolling his eyes to himself as both Lord and Lady Yardley turned their attention towards him. Flushing, he shrugged. "I suppose I would count myself as someone who does not believe such a thing to have any importance. I may not even believe in the concept!"

Lady Yardley's eyes opened wide.

"You mean to say that what Lord Yardley and I share is something you do not believe in?"

Blinking rapidly, Jonathan tried to explain, his chest suddenly tight.

"No, it is not that I do not believe it a meaningful connection which can be found between two people such as yourselves. It is that I personally have no interest in it. I have no intention of marrying someone simply because I find myself in love with them. In truth, I do not know if I am even capable of such a feeling."

"I can assure you that you are, whether or not you believe yourself to be."

Lord Yardley muttered his remark rather quietly and

Jonathan took in a slow breath, praying that his friend would not start instructing him on the matter of love."

Lady Yardley smiled and gazed at Jonathan for some moments before taking a breath and continuing.

"All the same, I do want my cousin to be cautious, particularly during this evening's ball. I want her to understand that not every gentleman will be as she expects."

"I am sure such gentlemen will make that obvious all by themselves."

This brought a frown to Lady Yardley's features, but a chuckle came from Lord Yardley instead. Jonathan grinned, just as the door opened and a young lady stepped into the room, beckoned by Lady Yardley. A gentle smile softened her delicate features as she glanced around the room, her eyes finally lingering on Jonathan.

"I feel as though I have walked into something most mysterious since everyone stopped talking the moment I entered." One eyebrow arching, she smiled at him. "I do hope that someone will tell me what it is all about!"

Jonathan rose, as was polite, but his lips seemed no longer able to deliver speech. Even his breath seemed to have fixed itself inside his chest as he stared, his mouth ajar, at the beautiful young woman who had just walked in. Her skin was like alabaster, her lips a gentle pink, pulled into a soft smile as blue eyes sparkled back at him. He had nothing to say and everything to say at the very same time. Could this delightful young woman be Lady Yardley's cousin? And if she was, then why was no one introducing him?

"Allow me to introduce you." As though he had read his thoughts, Lord Yardley threw out one hand towards the young woman. "Might I present Lady Cassandra, daughter to the Earl of Holford. And this, Lady Cassandra, is my dear friend, the Marquess of Sherbourne. He is an excellent sort. You need have no fears with him."

Bowing quickly towards the young woman, Jonathan fought to find his breath.

"I certainly would not be so self-aggrandizing as to say that I was 'an excellent sort', Lady Cassandra." he was somehow unable to draw his gaze away from her, and his heart leaped in his chest when she smiled all the more. "But I shall be the most excellent companion to you, should you require it, just as I am with Lord and Lady Yardley."

There was a breath of silence, and Jonathan cleared his throat, aware that he had just said more to her than he had ever said to any other young lady upon first making their acquaintance. Even Lord Yardley appeared to be a little surprised, for there was a blink, a smile and, after another long pause, the conversation continued. Lady Yardley gestured for her cousin to come and sit beside her, and the young lady obliged. Jonathan finally managed to drag his eyes away to another part of the room, only just becoming aware of how frantically his heart was beating. Everything he had just said to his friend regarding what would occur should he ever meet a young lady who stole his attention in an instant came back to him. Had he meant those words?

Giving himself a slight shake, Jonathan settled back into his chair, lost in thought as conversation flowed around the room. This was nothing more than an instant attraction, the swift kick of desire which would be gone within a few hours. There was nothing of any seriousness in such a swift response, he told himself. He had nothing to concern himself with and thus, he tried to insert himself back into the conversation just as quickly as he could.

. . .

Oh, no, Jonathan likes her! Perhaps he will have to change his mind about becoming leg-shackled! Check out the rest of story in the Kindle Store The Heart of a Gentleman

Join my Mailing List

Sign up for my newsletter to stay up to date on new releases, contests, giveaways, freebies, and deals!

Free book with signup!

Monthly Facebook Giveaways! Books and Amazon gift cards!
Join me on Facebook: https://www.facebook.com/ rosepearsonauthor

Website: www.RosePearsonAuthor.com

Follow me on Goodreads: Author Page

Printed in Dunstable, United Kingdom